ANISHA
ACCIDENTAL DETECTIVE

KU-315-201

SERENA PATEL

Illustrated by **Emma McCann**

CHAPTER ONE

HALLOWEEN!

Our school is doing the most **AWFUL** thing ever. Worse than PE out in the freezing cold, worse than listening to Mr Graft our head teacher in assembly last thing on a Friday, worse than soggy green beans for school dinners. We're having a **school disco**!

I don't like this idea for **several** reasons:

1. Disco = dancing (enough said!)
2. It's a themed disco for Halloween – which means everyone's already started acting wild and trying to scare each other. So annoying!
3. We haven't had a school disco for ten years, because the last time we had one apparently

it all went very wrong. Er, hello, why bring it back then?

The disco is this Friday and it's all anyone is talking about. We're doing the preparations this week, so it means some of our normal lessons are off while we try to make our school look **SPOOKY**. If you ask me, there's already a fair number of dusty old cobwebs in the corners of the rooms, so I don't see why we need to do much more. But the teachers are insisting we make posters in our art lesson! Even maths wasn't safe this morning – Mr Helix had us calculating the number of cheese twists we need for the party!

Mr Graft has been up into the school loft which no one ever goes into and brought down a box of old Halloween stuff, including a very rickety-looking skeleton who is apparently called Fred. One of the boys from the year below got hold of Fred and started dancing around with him. Mr Graft was **NOT** impressed. Some of the other boys also got into trouble for wrapping each other in toilet roll and pretending to be mummies. It's going to be a long week!

"Aren't you a little excited, Neesh?" Milo asks me as we walk to our class for afternoon registration.

"Not really, Milo. Nothing ever runs smoothly round here and the disco is already making everyone act **really silly**. Imagine what it'll be like on the day! I'm kind of glad it's straight after school – I might just go home and not stay for it."

"You can't do that! I was hoping we could dress up together. I thought we could go as Spookbusters

– you know, with the boiler suits and backpacks and ghost-zappers." He grins.

I laugh. "I'll think about it. Come on, let's get to class."

When we reach our classroom, Beena Bhatt is aggressively pushing sparkly gold envelopes into everyone's hands. She's got her two besties, Layla and Amani, following her around as usual.

She stops in front of us, looks us up and down and then sighs. "Well, I suppose you two are invited as well," she says, and shoves envelopes into our hands.

Milo and I look at each other quizzically. What could it be? I sit down and open mine as Mr Helix does the register.

It's an invitation!

It says:

YOU ARE INVITED TO THE BIRTHDAY PARTY OF

Miss Beena Bhatt

ON FRIDAY 31ST OCTOBER

AT THE SAPPHIRE BANQUETING SUITE
4 P.M. TO 6 P.M.

DRESS CODE: PARTYWEAR – NO HALLOWEEN COSTUMES!

ENTERTAINMENT: THE GHOULS – THE ONLINE SINGING SENSATIONS

BE THERE OR BE BORING!

Wow, this is possibly the most intimidating party invite I've ever received – but then it is from Beena Bhatt.

"Beena!" Milo shouts out as he realizes something.

"What?" she snaps.

"The invite says your party is this Friday? But that's the same day as—"

"Yes, yes, I know, the stupid spooky disco. My party is going to be **SO** much better though. Didn't you read the invitation? My mum has booked The Ghouls."

Milo looks blank.

Beena sighs loudly. "Oh, well I wouldn't expect you to know who they are. They're uber-cool and you're, well, *not*, are you?"

Milo ignores her insult. "Well, I think I'll be going to the spooky disco – I wanted to dress up. But have a nice time at your party," he says brightly.

Beena scowls. "Suit yourself," she says, and she marches over and snatches his invite away! She looks at me. "I suppose you'll be doing what he does since you two are always stuck together."

"Well, I wasn't planning to do either. I don't really like getting dressed up or going to big parties – too many people!" I say.

"Urgh, boring! Fine, your loss!" Beena says, snatching my invite out of my hand too. She really can be vile sometimes.

"Anyone else going to be total losers and miss out on the party of the year?" Beena asks the room, even though Mr Helix is still taking the register. A few kids hand their invitations back to her and the rest just look scared and say nothing or look out the window.

"Beena, maybe your social life could wait till afternoon break," Mr Helix says sternly.

Beena stomps back to her desk and slumps in

her chair. She looks annoyed but, more than that, she looks a bit...sad. She catches me looking at her and glares back. Okay, no, she's not sad, just her usual annoyed, obnoxious self then.

At afternoon break, Milo, Mindy, Manny and I catch up. Mindy and Manny agree they'd rather go to the spooky disco too and they all pester me until I promise I'll come along.

Milo is so excited. "Can we all go as Spookbusters? All four of us would look so cool dressed the same. My nan will help with the costumes. It'll be fun – I promise, Neesh!"

I laugh. "Milo Moon, the things I do for our friendship."

Mindy nudges me playfully. "Yay! We're going to make this the **best** spooky disco ever."

"**Spookbusters rule!**" Manny shouts.

CHAPTER TWO

BIG NEWS!

When I get home that afternoon, there's a car I don't recognize in the driveway. Do we have a guest? I let myself in and straight away I hear Mum and Dad talking to someone. I pop my head round the living-room door. Oh, it's Beena Bhatt's mum! What is she doing here?

"Oh, sweetheart, we lost track of time, we thought we'd be done before you got home..." Mum says nervously, glancing at Dad. "You know Mrs Bhatt, don't you? I think her daughter is in your class, isn't she?"

"Yeah, Beena," I say, looking suspiciously at

Mrs Bhatt, who is holding a clipboard. There's also a brochure on the coffee table which has a picture of a house on it.

"What's going on?" I ask.

Beena's mum smiles at me and then turns to Mum and Dad. "I think I have everything I need; I'll be in touch later in the week, okay?" she says, getting up and grabbing her bag. "Anisha, I'll see you very soon, hopefully at Beena's party on Friday. You will be there, won't you? It would mean the world to Beena, I'm sure."

I just smile and say nothing – clearly Beena's mum has no idea what her darling Beena is **REALLY** like!

When Mrs Bhatt has left, I look at Mum and Dad. "Why was she here?"

"Well, we need to talk to you, sweetheart," Mum starts. "We have wonderful news."

Just then Granny Jas comes in. "Pah, wonderful, my foot! The rest of you can do what you want, I'm not going anywhere!"

"Who's going somewhere?" I ask.

"Not **ME**!" says Granny as she sits down on the sofa, folding her arms and glaring at Mum and Dad. I've never seen her so angry!

"Can someone please tell me what's going on?" I ask.

Just then Aunty Bindi barges in, holding her laptop in one hand and a big binder in the other. "I need to use your Wi-Fi!" she says. "Ours is down and I have this really important research to do. You don't mind, do you? Tony and the kids are coming as well. I told them we might as well eat here today."

Granny harrumphs. "Since when do you research anything? And this isn't a restaurant, you know; you can't just turn up and expect to be fed. How do you know I've cooked today?"

"Haven't you? Oh, we can order in then," Bindi says.

Granny rolls her eyes. "No, no. I'll put some potato and chickpeas on. Don't waste money on takeaways! Home-cooked food is better for you anyway."

Mindy and Manny walk in with Uncle Tony. The twins drop their bags and go straight to grab snacks from the kitchen, with Granny yelling "Wash your hands first!" at them.

"You alright, Anisha?" Uncle Tony asks, plonking himself next to me on the small sofa.

"I'm not sure," I say, staring at the brochure on the table. "Beena Bhatt's mum was here when I got home – and I've got a bad feeling about it."

"Beena Bhatt's mum? Is she the estate agent?" Aunty Bindi asks as she opens up her laptop.

Dad blinks nervously. "Um, yes, that's her. We, um, just wanted to have a chat with her."

"About what?" I ask uneasily.

The twins come in from the kitchen and stand in the doorway.

"Yes, share your ridiculous plan, **beta**!" Granny tells Dad.

Dad gulps. "Well, we've lived in this house for a long time now and we thought it might be nice to have a bit more space. In a new house."

My tummy dips. Did I just hear that right? The room is silent. "A **new house**? But we live here, we have this house. Why would we move? And to where?" I ask. All the while, my heart is thudding in my chest.

"There's a new housing development on the other side of the city," Mum says, smiling. "It's lovely – we'd have a spare room for sleepovers and an office for your dad and me to work in. I've been thinking of doing an evening course and I could do with a space to study in. You'd have a bigger bedroom too, Anisha!"

They're actually serious about this. I feel sick.

"I don't want a bigger bedroom; I like my bedroom here!" It comes out louder than I meant it to.

"See!" Granny points at me triumphantly. "I knew she'd hate the idea too."

"If you moved, would Anisha still come to our school?" Mindy asks quietly.

Mum looks at Dad again. "Well, no, it would be a bit too far, so we'd need to look at a school that side of the city. There are some really nice ones."

I look at Mindy, who looks like she's going to cry. "Yeah, but my friends aren't at those schools," I say. This can't be happening.

"No, but you'd make new friends," Dad says. "And your family will still be your family. You'll see Mindy, Manny and even Milo at the weekends."

"I don't want new friends or a new bedroom or a new house," I say. "Call Beena's mum and tell her it's not going to happen. We're not moving."

"But we already told her we want to sell this house. She's putting it on their website tomorrow,"

Mum says. "You'll see, Anisha, this will be a good thing for our family."

I look around the room. Mindy and Manny look gutted, Granny Jas looks furious, Uncle Tony looks at his feet and Aunty Bindi looks like she wants to throw up.

CHAPTER THREE

THINGS GET SPOOKY!

I spend the rest of the evening in my room with Mindy and Manny, discussing how we can stop the move from happening.

"I could chain myself to the house and block the door so you can't leave," Manny offers. "Oh, but then what if I need a wee – or, worse, what if I get hungry? Wait, I know, we could make really bad smells all over the house so when potential buyers come to look at it, they get put off!"

"It's putting me off from sitting next to you," Mindy says in disgust as she moves away from him. "Anisha, what if you talk to your parents, explain how much you want to stay here?"

I shrug. "It seems like they've pretty much made up their minds. They think they're doing this **FOR** me!"

"Parents! They always think they know best." Mindy sighs.

Manny jumps up. "I've got it! We'll get Milo to hang around outside and tell people the house is haunted! Then when people say there's a boy outside telling everyone this house is haunted, we can say, 'What boy? There's been no boy living here for a hundred years!' They'll be so scared they'll run away!"

Mindy glares at him. "Manny, that is the daftest idea I've ever heard. It makes no sense! There are loads of kids living on this street. Just stop, this is serious – we need to come up with a plan that will actually work."

Manny looks upset for a second but then grins. "We can pretend the **WHOLE** street is haunted! I'm going to draw up a plan of all the houses and make a list of what we'll need."

Mindy puts her face in her hands. "Oh, brother!"

"I'm really going to have to move, aren't I?" I say. "But I can't imagine living anywhere except here. It would be so weird – not waking up in my room, not having breakfast in my kitchen, not walking down the road and meeting Milo or seeing you guys at school. It wouldn't be right!"

"We'll figure something out, Anisha, we will," Mindy promises, putting her hand on mine. "Hey, how about if you came and lived with us?"

"I would, but I'll miss my parents and I definitely can't leave Granny Jas," I say. "We have to find another way."

"I can't believe they want to move. I thought you guys were happy here," Manny says.

"So did I!" I reply. "I don't know what's got into them. They get these weird ideas and everyone else has to go along with it. It's like when Dad decided he wanted to see if he could give up his car and roller-skate everywhere – and he ended up skating into next-door's brand-new SUV. He left a big dent too! Oh, and the time Mum watched a thing about the new trend to add cauliflower to every meal because it's supposed to be good for you, and she made me cauliflower pizza! **Yuk!**"

"Wow, they do have a lot of bad ideas," Mindy agrees. "Well, hopefully they'll realize this one is a bad idea before you actually have to move anywhere."

"I hope so!" I say...but I'm not convinced.

We agree to leave it for tonight and talk tomorrow. But when I get into bed later there are still too many thoughts going round in my head about what it would mean if we move. I can't relax, so I decide to finish my book. I've been reading this amazing series and I can't wait to get the next one out from the school library. I stay up way too late though and the next morning I'm dragging myself downstairs, exhausted.

To my surprise there is chaos in the kitchen. Granny seems to be pulling out every single utensil, pot and plate we own. Everything is everywhere! And I mean **everywhere**! There's a pile of dishes on the counter that looks very unstable. I also notice we seem to own a lot of rolling pins and the biggest cooking pot I've ever seen.

"Granny, what are you doing?" I ask.

"Oh, morning, beta! I'm packing," she answers cheerfully.

"I thought you didn't want to move. *I* don't want to move," I say, worried. "We're not moving right now, are we?"

"Ha, don't panic, beta, this is all part of my plan to make your parents see what a mistake they're making. They don't realize how much work it is to pack everything and then find it all again afterwards. I thought I would give them a little taste by packing up some of the kitchen. I've already hidden your father's favourite mug. He can't have his morning coffee in any other cup. He's going to be so annoyed!" she chuckles.

"Granny, you're an **evil genius**!" I say.

"Granny always has a plan." She taps her nose and winks at me. I can't help but smile.

"Anyway," she continues, "you can't be worrying about this, you have an exciting week. That Halloween disco is coming up, isn't it? I seem to remember something in the newsletter they send home."

"**Urgh**, don't remind me," I say. "Everyone thinks this spooky party is going to be so fantastic."

"But you don't?" Granny asks.

"It's just, well, discos...dancing – not really my thing," I reply.

"Ooh, I used to love a good disco-dance. You know, your grandfather was quite a mover." Granny grins.

I screw up my face, trying to imagine my grandparents dancing. Nope, it's too weird!

"What is that look you're giving me? I wasn't always your granny, you know! I was young and hip and quite **groovy** actually," Granny scolds. "Now, off to school with you! I have things to do and mess to make!"

I pick up Milo on the walk to school and fill him in on my parents' plan to move. He stops in the middle of the street.

"**WHAT**? They can't, Neesh! We've always lived near each other!"

"I know, Milo, I don't **WANT** to move. It's the worst idea they've ever come up with," I moan.

"There's got to be something we can do," Milo says.

"Manny already came up with a bunch of plans – not good ones though. Granny says she'll handle it, but I'm not sure even she can fix this," I admit. "What if she makes it worse?"

Milo grins. "Don't worry, Neesh. If Granny Jas is on the case, she'll find a way to make everything better."

"I hope so, Milo," I say. "I really do."

We soon forget our problems when we get into school, because the Halloween hype has been turned up by several levels. Kids have brought in decorations from home and there's lots of excitement about putting them up. Mr Graft is dancing Ghastly Gertrude, a floaty fake ghost he found in the Halloween box, up and down the hallways as everyone makes their way to their classrooms.

Our first lesson is science in the lab, so at least that's one good thing today. I notice Skeleton Fred is propped up on a stool at the front of the classroom. Mr Graft must have put him there as a joke. He loves all this Halloween stuff – he's been in such a good mood since they decided to put on the disco. Milo notices Miss Bunsen has brought in her pet snake Fang and goes over to his tank to say "hi". Miss brings him in from time to time – he's kind of the unofficial school pet.

The rest of the class pile in and we all sit down. Mindy and Manny sit just in front of Milo and me. Beena Bhatt plonks herself at the front closest to Fred. She's not waffling on about her party like she was yesterday – phew! Just then Miss Bunsen comes in, but she doesn't look like our usual Miss Bunsen. It's her hair...it's **GREEN**! Not just any green either, but bright luminescent green!

She notices us all staring and clears her throat loudly. "Yes, Year Six, my hair is green. I, um, was getting my costume ready for the disco and I thought I would dye my hair to complete the look. I may have left the dye on for a bit too long. Well, more than a bit. Okay, I fell asleep in it."

"It's **glowing**!" Beena snorts.

Miss Bunsen frowns. "Yes, thank you, Beena, it does have a slightly luminescent effect which makes it glow in the dark. I'm not sure why – it may be a reaction with my hairspray." She pats her hair nervously. "Anyway, it's a good example of the things to be aware of when using chemicals! Now, shall we get on with our morning?"

Before we can start our lesson though, Mr Graft comes in holding a big box of craft stuff and plonks it on the desk in front of Miss Bunsen. He winces a bit when he sees her hair but doesn't comment.

"Morning, Miss Bunsen. Morning, class. Instead of your usual lesson, I thought you could assist with decoration-making for the disco. It's a big event and I need all fangs on deck!" he declares proudly.

"See what I did there? It should be 'hands' but I said 'fangs' – you know, like a vampire, because it's Halloween!" He grins.

Everyone groans at the terrible joke.

"But, sir, we're not on a ship though, we're in a classroom," someone shouts out.

Mr Graft glares as he tries to see who said that. "It's just a phrase. I'm well aware we are in a classroom, thank you! Now why don't you get on with the task in hand?"

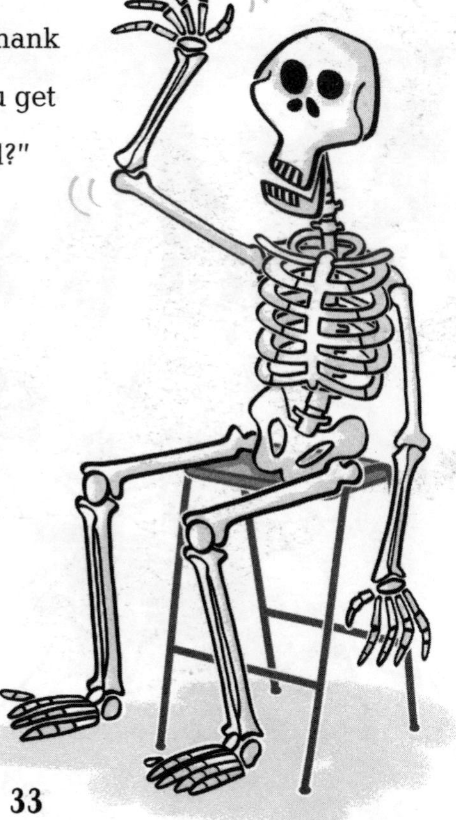

He turns to leave, but just as he does the strangest thing happens. Out of the corner of my eye I see Skeleton Fred's arm move. It lifts up, all by itself! The lights flicker and everyone gasps.

Then eerie music comes out of the speakers on the board at the front of the classroom. It even makes me jump! Mr Graft steps back as Skeleton Fred points at the board, which suddenly lights up…and there on the screen it says **BOO!**

Someone screams and Milo nudges me as we all gawp at what's happening in our classroom.

"What on earth?" Mr Graft shouts.

Miss Bunsen looks around the room. "Is this someone's idea of a joke?"

But then Skeleton Fred shakes his head as if he's saying no!

Miss Bunsen staggers backwards and falls into her chair. Then, as if it never happened, the board switches off, the music stops and Fred is limp again.

The class erupts into chaos. Everyone is shouting.

"Woah, did you see that?"

"Fred moved!"

"The school is haunted!'

Mr Graft tries to regain control but it's no good, everyone saw it.

Milo leans over. "That was so cool! Do you think the school is actually haunted? We might get to catch a real ghost!"

"It was probably just a power surge. Or Fred got knocked by something, or someone is having a joke. I don't believe in **ghosts**," I say, rubbing the goosebumps that are still on my arms.

"Yeah, but that was pretty convincing. Did you see how Skeleton Fred came to life, Neesh?"

"Come on, think about what you're saying. Came to life? It's probably just our eyes playing tricks on us, Milo. He doesn't look very stable, does he? His arm probably just fell," I say, trying to convince myself.

Milo raises an eyebrow sceptically. "Upwards?"

Once everyone calms down, Miss Bunsen switches off the board at the plug socket. Mr Graft does a little check around Fred for any controls or strings that might have been used by someone to make the skeleton move, but he doesn't spot anything.

"If I find out that one of you was behind that little stunt there will be trouble, mark my words!" he warns before he leaves. "I'll be keeping my eye on all of you!" Then he does that cringey thing where he points at his own eyes and then at all of us to show he's watching.

Everyone is still chatting about what happened while we get on with making decorations. Milo and I make streamers in orange and green. I prefer a proper science lesson but, as activities go, it's not the worst thing. Mindy and Manny make Halloween bunting out of old scraps of felt. Some of the other kids make a huge banner saying *Happy Halloween*.

Beena folds her arms and refuses to take part because, as she says, "This disco is going to be lame and my party will be much better." She then

proceeds to tell Miss Bunsen all about the band she's booked, The Ghouls. Miss Bunsen looks bored but listens, then sneakily hands Beena a pair of scissors and gets her to cut out ghost shapes. Beena is so busy talking she doesn't realize she's helping out now.

Towards the end of the lesson Miss Bunsen lets the class help feed Fang. I'm not usually into reptiles but I don't mind him. He's kind of goofy for a snake and sometimes ties himself in knots that he can't get out of. Milo adores him of course. Some of the kids are a bit frightened, but Miss Bunsen explains that snakes are quite docile unless they feel threatened. Even Beena has a turn holding him, which surprises me.

"I'm going to ask my mum if I can have a pet snake," Milo declares.

"Ha, you've got more chance of getting a pet horse, Milo." Mindy laughs. "You already have a lobster and a rat, remember? Plus, snakes eat rats, don't they?"

Milo looks horrified. "Mine wouldn't! They'd be friends! I'd make sure of it!" he insists.

"Of course you would, Milo." Miss Bunsen smiles.

Just then the bell goes for break. We tidy up and put Fang back in his tank.

"What an eventful start to the week we've had," Miss Bunsen says. "Hopefully the rest of the day will be much calmer."

"I wouldn't count on it, miss!" someone jokes.

I feel a cold shiver down my spine again. I look over at Skeleton Fred, who is still lifeless and floppy. Definitely not haunted. Definitely **NOT**. Right?

CHAPTER FOUR

GHOST IN THE LIBRARY!

When everyone heads out for break, I hang back for a moment until the classroom is empty. I walk over to Skeleton Fred; he's just propped on the stool, limp and lifeless. Did we really see him point at the board? I lift his arm up. Nothing. I check for anything unusual that might suggest someone had messed with him, but it's just Fred – no secret controls or buttons. Could he really have come to life?

No, don't be silly, Anisha. Because skeletons don't come to life. How could they?

"Behave yourself!" I tell Skeleton Fred as I leave the class. What am I doing talking to a skeleton?

Wow, all this Halloween silliness must be getting to me!

I head outside. It's break time and news soon spreads through the playground about what happened in the science lab. Some of the younger boys run around chasing each other, pretending to be ghosts and zombies. Manny and Milo get into character as Spookbusters and go investigating around the wooden fitness trail, even though there's nothing there but ropes and wooden posts to climb on.

"Everyone's really getting into all this Halloween stuff, aren't they?" Mindy comments as she bites into her apple.

"Yeah, it's like they *want* the school to be haunted," I say.

"Ha, they're just excited for the disco. Anyway, we have bigger things to worry about. What's the latest on stopping this house move?" Mindy asks.

"Granny's pretending to go along with it for now but she has a plan to make it as difficult as possible," I reply. "You know what Granny Jas is like – if she doesn't want to do something, then it's not happening. I trust Granny, I just hope she can sort it."

"**Yesss**! Granny is awesome. I'll see if she needs any help after school. I think we're coming to yours again. Our Wi-Fi is still down and Bindi has some project she's working on but won't tell us about. She just keeps muttering about a countdown."

"I hope she's not planning anything for

Halloween," I say. "This school stuff is enough already!"

"It's just hype. People will get bored of it soon," Mindy says. "No one really believes in ghosts."

"You should," a voice behind us says.

I turn to see who it is. It's Maryam from the other class in our year. She looks around and then continues, "You know the school is haunted, right?"

I laugh. "Don't be silly, Maryam. There's no such thing as ghosts."

Maryam looks horrified. "Don't mock what you don't understand, Anisha! Haven't you heard the stories about the last spooky disco they held here?"

Mindy looks intrigued. "No, what happened?"

Maryam leans in close. "Well, my big sister used to go here, and she told me that the reason they stopped having discos is because of what happened in her last year."

"What happened?" I ask impatiently as Milo and Manny stop running around and come to listen too.

"Well, they say the ghost of the first head teacher of this school used to roam the corridors looking for children to tell off. When he was alive, he hated any sort of celebration and he swore he would never leave his position of head teacher so he could make sure pupils always followed his rules. And so when he died, they say he came back to haunt the school. On the night of the last Halloween disco, he made the lights flicker, blew the sound system and turned all the food to slime! The disco was ruined, and my sister said everyone who was there ran screaming from the hall. So, the board of governors – they're the big bosses around here – decided it couldn't ever be allowed to happen again. Until now!" she finishes darkly. "I don't know why they're ignoring the horror of the past but, if you ask me, it's a **BIG MISTAKE** having this disco."

As she walks off, I look at Mindy. "She's a bit intense, isn't she?"

"Do you think it's true, Neesh?" Milo asks. "I've never seen a ghost before. But I watched a documentary once where this man tried talking to spirits in a haunted house. If there's a real ghost, maybe we could talk to it, see if we can help it."

"Milo, firstly, why are you watching stuff like that? Secondly, you can't help a ghost." I shake my head. "What am I saying? There's no such thing! Maryam's story makes no sense at all. Why haven't we seen or heard from this ghost before? We've been in this school for six whole years and this is the first time we're being told about it. I've never heard anything so silly. It's just one of those rumours that gets bigger and dafter with each new person who tells it."

Milo looks disappointed. "Yeah, you're probably right. It would be cool though!"

After break there's a meeting in the library for anyone in Year Six who wants to help organize the disco. Mindy, Milo and Manny all want to go, so I agree to join them. It's that or PE, and I prefer the warm library to doing laps of the field opposite our school in the cold.

Quite a lot of kids turn up for the meeting and we have to squish up sitting on the floor. I notice Beena at the back of the room with her two minions, Layla and Amani. She's flicking through a magazine. She doesn't even want to go to the disco, so why is she here? She probably just wanted to get out of PE too.

I make a mental note to get a book out before we leave – that new one in the series I've been reading. I wave at the librarian, Mr Bound, and he smiles back.

Mr Graft arrives then and stands at the front of the room, looking very serious. But he's also wearing a T-shirt over his normal shirt and tie that says **STAY WEIRD** in slime-style writing, so it is hard to take him completely seriously.

"Firstly, children, after this morning's events in the science lab I want to clear up any rumours that this school is haunted. Yes, we had a small, unexplained incident, but I am confident that it was some technical problem and it won't happen again. The Halloween disco is going to be a success, is that understood? We will not have a repeat of the issues that occurred some years ago. It's taken a long time for the school governors to agree to let us hold another disco, so let's not let them or ourselves down, okay?"

Everyone nods and says, "Yes, Mr Graft."

He smiles then and his mood seems to lift. "Right, let's discuss our party plans. First up are refreshments and snacks for the disco."

Someone shouts out, "Can we have candyfloss?" Someone else says, "Those cheesy string things!"

Then, "Ooh, what about spaghetti that looks like brains or intestines?"

"Eww, that's too gross!"

"Fruit juice but mix all the different flavours so it looks like a potion!"

Mr Graft gestures for quiet. "Hands up, please, no shouting out."

But before he or anyone else can say anything more, the lights in the library begin to flicker. I feel like something weird is about to happen again.

Suddenly a book goes whooshing over our heads and across the room, just missing Mr Graft's face! He flinches and the book lands with a thud on the floor behind him.

Everyone gasps, including me. I can't believe what just happened!

"What on earth? WHO DID THAT?" Mr Graft shouts. "I demand to know **NOW!**"

There's silence – and then another book comes flying from the back of the room, narrowly missing the librarian Mr Bound's head. He squeals and ducks down.

Then a third book *and* a fourth book come flying past us, hitting the walls with loud cracks. I try to see who is throwing the books or where they're coming from, but there's too much commotion. At which point Mr Graft shouts, "Right, everyone out! **EVACUATE!**"

There's panic and pushing and shoving as we leave the library. Two more books whizz past as we shuffle out.

Mr Bound is huffing and puffing as he locks the door behind him.

"I don't know what just happened but that was not normal! THE LIBRARY IS CLOSED UNTIL FURTHER NOTICE! I lived through the last haunting and it was **NO JOKE**, let me tell you.

It's taken this long for my nerves to settle. I'm not sticking around for a second ghost attack," he shouts and runs away.

"What?" I cry. "It can't be! And I didn't get my book yet! It seems a bit drastic to close the library, sir!"

Mr Graft pats my shoulder. "Flying books are a matter of health and safety. Now, I'm not saying there's a real ghost haunting the school, but I'm afraid Mr Bound is right; the library has to remain closed until we can figure out what's going on. Obviously, there are no such things as ghosts and there's nothing to be scared of – we just have to get to the bottom of it all,"

he says. He's looking around and above him suspiciously, until he seems to realize something. "Oh, no! The board of governors will be horrified when they hear about this. I need to go and do some damage control. Get to lessons, everyone!" And he hurries away, muttering to himself.

"He's being so weird lately," I say.

"He's always been weird," Mindy jokes.

"Well, weird or not, closing the library is harsh." I sulk. "And now we have to do PE as well, extra harsh!"

Everyone starts to move away and go back to their classrooms.

"I was willing to write off the thing with the skeleton as a silly prank. Plus, no one got hurt that time. But this is next level," I say. "Making it seem like the school is haunted for Halloween is one thing, but throwing books and having the library shut down – well, that's just not on. So disrespectful!"

"What can we do though, Anisha? I mean, you

have to admit, that was kind of spooky. What if Maryam is right and there *is* a ghost of a past head teacher?" Mindy shivers.

Milo and Manny join us, all excited. "That was **awesome**!" they say together.

"I'm not sure it would have been so awesome if one of those flying books had bopped you on the nose!" Mindy tells them.

Manny ignores her. "Wait till I tell Dad about this – he's going to freak out! The disco is going to be even more amazing if it has a real ghost!"

"Or the disco will get cancelled because parents won't want their kids coming if they think there's a ghost on the loose!" I say.

Milo looks worried. "You're right. Mr Graft already said nothing else could go wrong and they have to make sure everything runs smoothly. What if they cancel the disco, Neesh? No Spookbusters, no fizzy pop, no showing off my best moves on the dance floor!"

"We won't let that happen, Milo," I reply firmly.

"But, I thought you hated discos, Neesh?" Milo asks.

I shrug. "I do, but...the whole moving-house thing has made me look at it all differently. If I move away then I'll never get to be part of anything at this school again – this could be my first and last school disco with you all! So, I guess what I'm saying is that this is more important to me than I thought. I care about our school and now I care about the disco too. We have to stop this fake ghost and save the party!"

"Hooray!" Milo cheers. "And don't worry, we're not going to let you move anywhere. But first, let's stop this spook!"

I smile. "You know, Milo, we might need the Spookbusters after all. Now, what do you actually know about catching ghosts?" I ask.

CHAPTER FIVE

SPOOK-VESTIGATIONS

It turns out that Milo and Manny don't know very much about catching ghosts apart from what they've seen on telly. Since we don't have access to proton packs and ghost-trap box thingies, we're a bit stuck. Not that I think we're dealing with a real ghost but, you know, it doesn't hurt to be prepared.

"The problem is we don't know where it's going to strike next. We need a clue, something that will help us figure out who's behind it all," I say.

"Well, it could be someone in our year group. The first thing happened in our science lab and the second time was in the library with only people from

Year Six present," Mindy points out.

"Okay, good, we've got a starting point," I say. "Now we need to think about who would want everyone to think the school was haunted. Could it just be a Halloween joke? Everyone's so excited this week, perhaps they think it's funny?"

"Yeah, but throwing books across the library is a bit extra, Anisha. Anyone who's met Mr Graft would know he won't find that funny. And he did warn everyone about messing about after the science lab incident."

"Okay, well maybe if we get a look inside the library, we might find a clue as to what's going on," I say. "There was nothing in the science lab, but hopefully we'll see something there."

"It's locked though. Mr Bound said it's closed until further notice," Milo says.

"We'll come back later," I say. "I know where there might be a spare key to the library. In the meantime, let's get to PE. Hopefully we're not playing dodge ball – I always get hit in the head and it really hurts, even with the soft ball!"

The rest of the morning is thankfully uneventful. PE is okay for once: no dodge ball! We have a normal but boring geography lesson followed by English and then it's time for lunch. Before we go to the canteen I grab Milo, Mindy and Manny and lead them to Mr Bristles's office. He's the caretaker of our school.

"Why are we here?" Milo asks.

"Mr Bristles has spare keys for all the rooms in school. He'll have one for the library," I say.

"Brilliant idea!" Mindy grins.

I knock on the door – no answer. I push the door slightly and it opens. I breathe a sigh of relief, even though I'm not thrilled about sneaking in. Mr Bristles must be out and about doing jobs around the school and forgot to lock his office. I point to the little metal cabinet on the wall where he keeps the spare keys. "I'm hoping it's in there," I say.

Manny pulls the door to the cabinet open – there are so many keys! Luckily they all have blue tags with labels on them. Manny grabs the one that says *Library* on it, passes it to me and we turn to leave.

"Looking for me?" says Mr Bristles, who is standing in the doorway.

"Um, no...I mean, yes!" I say, holding my hand behind my back.

"Is it no or is it yes?" Mr Bristles frowns and looks around his room.

Mindy jumps in front of me. "It's yes. We wondered if you'd answer some questions for the school blog. We're interviewing a different member of staff every month. Only the important ones, obviously."

Mr Bristles blushes and smiles. "Well, I've got some more jobs to do now, but come back later and I'll clean myself up for a photo too."

"Lovely!" Mindy says brightly. "Come on, gang, let's go and get lunch and think up our questions for Mr Bristles."

"Are we really going to interview him?" Manny asks once we've left Mr Bristles. "We don't work on the school blog. Does the school even have a blog?"

"We just needed a reason why we were there. I had to think fast and make something up," Mindy says.

"I feel bad," I say. "He's going to spruce himself up for a photo."

"We'll say we've had a technical problem – he'll soon forget about it," Milo says.

"Let's get to the library and then to the canteen before lunch finishes – I'm starving!" Manny says.

"You're always starving," Mindy complains. "We're in the second sitting anyway…but actually, I am kind of hungry now too."

We race to the library where thankfully the corridor is quiet. I slip the key into the lock and turn it. My heart is pounding. I would never normally do this, but then the library has never been closed because of a suspected ghost before!

The door clicks open. It's dark in there. We step inside cautiously.

"I'm scared," Milo says.

"Spook-vestigators can't be scared," Manny reminds him. "Although I do wish we had a torch."

READ KNOW GROW
KEEP CALM AND READ ON
BOOKS SCAR YOUR PANTS OF
My Teacher is a Vampire!
Surpr Math
Spiders in my Lunchbox!

"We could just put the lights on, losers." Mindy sighs and flicks the switch.

"Oh yeah!" Milo grins. "That's better."

"Right, we don't have much time. Mr Bound could decide to pop in at any moment. Let's check out the area where the books fell first," I say, walking over to where the books still lie, face down, pages splayed.

"I don't get it. How did the books fly across the room like that?" Mindy asks.

I walk to the back of the room, where the books had seemed to come from. "There's a dark corner behind a shelf here," I say. "Someone could have been hiding."

There's a book on the floor, but as I bend down to pick it up, something else catches my eye. It's a Y-shaped piece of wood, about the same length as a thirty-centimetre ruler, with a piece of long elastic tied between the two short ends. Wait a minute! It's a home-made catapult!

Taking the catapult in one hand and the book in the other, I pull back the elastic, place the book into it, and release. It soars across the room!

"Woah, how did you do that with the book, Neesh?" Milo asks.

"With this," I say, holding up the catapult. "Which means it's a **person** who made the books fly across the room, **NOT** a ghost!" It's then that I notice an orange hair caught in the catapult's string. Maybe it's a clue to the person who used it?

"Look!" I exclaim. "A hair that might belong to the non-ghost!"

"Dastardly!" Manny says, impressed.

"Yeah, and not supernatural at all," Mindy remarks.

"Oh, so we're not going to catch a real spook then?" Milo complains.

"It doesn't look like it," I say. "But we do have to catch the person who did this – before the disco gets cancelled."

"Hopefully nothing else happens in the meantime," Mindy says.

"How much haunting can one fake ghost do anyway?" Milo jokes.

We slip back out of the library, looking around to make sure no one sees us. Milo and Manny press themselves against the walls and edge along the hallway.

"We're blending in," Manny whisper-shouts to explain.

"To what? The Year Four display on *Titanic*?" Mindy points out.

On the way to return the key to Mr Bristles's room, we bump into Mr Bound. He's carrying a net and a pair of binoculars.

"All okay, Mr Bound?" I ask, trying to sound completely innocent as we approach him.

"Yes, I'm taking a stand. I was scared earlier but then I realized, someone has to protect our library!

So, I'm going to sit there until this so-called ghost shows its face and I'm going to catch it!" he says proudly.

Mindy raises an eyebrow. "With a net and some binoculars?"

"Night-vision goggles," Mr Bound corrects her.

"Oh wow!" I say brightly. "Good luck, Mr Bound, we'll...erm...pop by later to check in on you."

Mr Bound salutes us and marches away in the direction of the library.

"He can't be serious." Mindy laughs.

"I think it's a great idea if there was a real ghost," Milo says. "I kind of feel bad there isn't now!"

CHAPTER SIX

FOOD FIGHT!

When we get to lunch, we see Mr Graft seems to have forgotten about the fact that we have a fake ghost on the loose and is happily selling tickets to the Halloween disco. He's got two chairs set up behind him with Ghastly Gertrude the ghost and Skeleton Fred sitting on them. Are they kind of like his entourage now?

He's wearing a bright blue wig and monster hands, which makes it quite difficult for him to handle the pound coins children are giving him in exchange for a ticket. I also see Beena Bhatt trying to convince a table of kids to come to her party instead. I hear the words "unmissable" and then "**SUIT YOURSELF, LOSERS!**" when the conversation doesn't go her way.

We grab our trays and join the queue for lunch.

"What are you going to have?" Milo asks me. "There's soup or fish."

"Um, I think I might try the soup," I say. "I don't really like fish much."

"Dad took us to this posh restaurant once where the fish still had their heads and their eyes were just staring up at me! Totally put me off fish," Manny agrees.

"I think I might become a vegetarian," Milo declares. "I love living things too much to eat them and I keep remembering some of my favourite foods are actually really lovely animals."

Just then we get to the front of the queue. I ask for soup but there's none left in the pot on the counter, so the dinner lady goes to get some more. She lifts another big pot from the cooker at the back and places it in front of her. She carefully lifts the lid, holding her ladle ready to dish some out, but when she sees what's inside she screams and knocks the whole pot to the floor! I gasp, thinking she's going to get burned by hot soup – but it's not hot and it's not soup. It's a big sloppy puddle of gloopy, gloppy green **SLIME! YUK!**

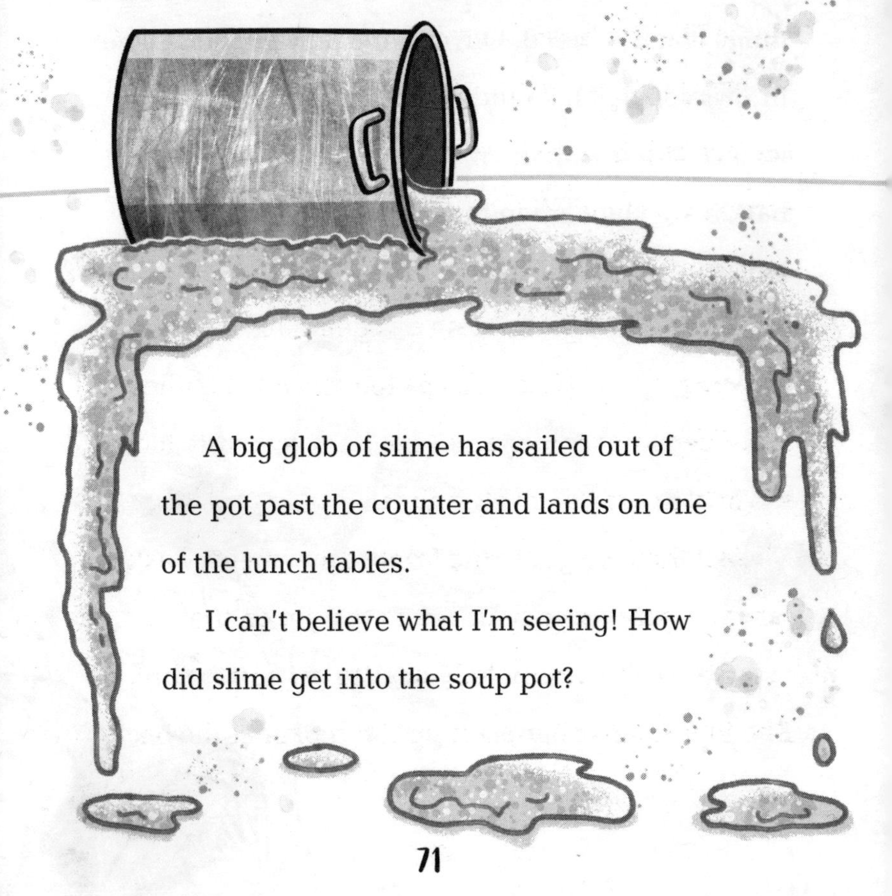

A big glob of slime has sailed out of the pot past the counter and lands on one of the lunch tables.

I can't believe what I'm seeing! How did slime get into the soup pot?

Milo and Manny shout, "**WOAH, SLIME!**" which obviously then gets the attention of a few people sitting nearby. I watch everything that happens next in slow motion, like it's a movie or something. It doesn't feel real.

First Micah from our class suddenly grabs a handful of the gloopy stuff from the lunch table and flings it at his friend, Oliver, for a laugh. Then Oliver throws some of his sandwich back at Micah. Keeley, who is sitting with them, laughs and throws a handful of slime up in the air. It lands in people's hair and on their plates.

Mr Graft sees what's happening at this point and comes over, shouting, "STOP that right now! No slime-throwing. Wait, where did the slime come from?" He's momentarily confused but doesn't watch his step and a big splodge of slime under his foot sends him flying across the floor. **OOF!**

Micah snorts and then shouts out, "**FOOD FIGHT!**" That just sends the whole canteen into chaos and kids start throwing slime and food at each other. Mindy and I crouch down by the counter. Manny and Milo duck under a table. I notice the dinner ladies are hiding too!

"Everyone's gone wild!" Mindy yells above the noise.

"What do we do?" Manny shouts.

"Stay here, they'll run out of things to throw soon. I hope!" I say as a splat of soup lands on the floor near me.

"Or…" Mindy grins. "We could join in!"

"No, are you joking? I don't think—" But before I can finish my sentence, Milo has smushed a splat of slime in Manny's hair and Manny is looking around for something to fling back at him.

Mindy laughs. "Come on, Anisha, when do WE ever do something like this? Don't you want to know what it feels like, just a little?"

I think for a moment. Everything HAS been really stressful lately – what with the house move and the fake haunting. I guess it would be nice to forget everything for a minute and it wouldn't really be hurting anyone…

Just then a blob of slime lands near me. I grab a handful – **gross**! It's cold and slimy! I throw it at Mindy, who catches it and hurls it back at me. It lands on my jumper and slides down. Mindy cackles.

I laugh. "Oh, so you think that's funny? Here, catch this!" I say, launching another glob of green slime right at her. I don't mean it to, but it lands right on her cheek and dribbles down her face.

"Oh, I'm sorry!" I say, but Mindy starts laughing. "See, this **IS** fun!"

Just when I'm thinking she's totally right, someone yells, "**SNAKE!**"

I look to where the scream came from. It's Maryam from the other class.

She's standing on her chair and staring, horrified, at the table where Fang, Miss Bunsen's pet snake, is slithering away!

"What on earth is Fang doing in here?" I say to Mindy, as Milo runs over, head ducked, to retrieve Fang. But Fang is not keen on being picked up! He slinks away quickly as Milo tries to get hold of him. Maryam is totally freaking out now, which makes the girl next to her freak out too. It's chaos!

Finally, Mr Graft manages to pick himself up. He looks around with horror, adjusts his blue wig and booms in his loudest, scariest voice for everyone to

We all stop what we're doing and stare at the mess in front of us. The canteen is destroyed! Slime on the tables, floor, people's faces, hair and clothes; plates and cups knocked over; food and drink spilled – just a big mess everywhere!

Mr Graft brushes the slime off his trousers, stands on a chair and gives us all a lecture then – something about history and the deeds of good men and not standing by while evil prevails. I'm not sure what it has to do with the food fight. To be honest, I'm only really half-listening, because I'm still wondering where the slime came from. That's what started all the food-throwing and it's not like slime is usually on the menu at our school. I mean, I know they serve us some disgusting-looking stuff sometimes, but slime is taking it a bit far. This fake ghost is really putting a lot of effort into making trouble around here. This is the third thing that's happened now and the pranks seem to be getting bigger each time. We have to stop whoever is doing this.

I make a mental note to speak to the dinner lady as soon as I can to see if she knows anything. Mr Graft finishes his speech and tells us all we have to stay here till the canteen is clean and everyone has to help. It gives me the chance I need. I pull Mindy's sleeve and beckon her to come with me.

We wait for Mr Graft to go to the other side of the hall. His earlier good mood has gone and he's barking orders at everyone. We quickly go round to the other side of the lunch counter, where the dinner ladies are muttering and trying to scoop up slime from the cooker and floor.

"Um, can we help?" I ask.

"Oh, yes please, dear," one dinner lady, Mrs Crust, replies. "I just don't understand how this happened. Slime! How did it even get in here? Mr Graft is mightily unhappy with us."

Mindy grabs a container from the side and we use a large spoon to scoop the slime into it.

"Who has access back here just before lunchtime?" I ask.

"No one apart from us. Sometimes Mr Graft comes in for a sneaky peek at the dinner menu and to take his lunch early, but apart from that I don't remember seeing anyone," Mrs Crust answers. "And where would they get so much slime from?"

I look around. "Well, there are a lot of containers back here. Could someone have hidden the slime in one of your pots sometime before and then just nipped in when your backs were turned and switched them?"

Mrs Crust frowns. "I suppose it's possible. We're usually so busy in that last half-hour before the lunch bell goes that we're in and out of the kitchen, fridge and pantry. Someone could do that when we weren't looking. But why? It's a terrible thing to do! And very unhygienic."

"That's what we have to figure out," I say. "I think it's all part of making the school seem haunted. You know, like in the movies when a ghost leaves a slimy trail."

"Oo-er, haunted, you say?" Mrs Crust gasps. "Well, I've heard the rumours of course."

Mindy pipes up then. "They're just that, Mrs Crust – rumours. Someone is messing with us all, making us think it's a ghost doing all this, but it's not."

"That's right," I say. "And we're going to find out exactly who that someone is."

Milo comes over then with Fang wrapped around his arm. "I'm going to take this little fella back to

Miss Bunsen's room,"
he says. "She's
probably worried
about where he's
got to. I wonder how
he managed to escape
his tank."

"Maybe someone let him out?" Manny says as he joins us.

"On purpose? It did freak everyone out. Maybe another tactic by our fake ghost?" I say.

"We still don't have a suspect though," Manny says.

I look around the room. It could be anyone here.

"It's most likely someone from our year, isn't it?" Milo points out.

"All the incidents so far have happened when our year has been present," I agree. "Our class were the only ones in the science lab when Fred pointed at the board and it switched on by itself.

But I guess someone from another class could still have set it up?"

At that moment Maryam comes over. She makes a point of not standing near Milo.

"That thing makes me feel all wibbly," she says, nodding at Fang.

"Aw, he's harmless really. Do you want to stroke him?" Milo asks.

"Ew, no!" Maryam squeals. "I came over to ask if you believe me now about the ghost of the school? Too many things have happened – you have to admit, it's **creepy**. It's him, the ghost of the first head teacher!"

"Maryam, I don't think it is," I say. "If ghosts were real – which they're not – would they haunt in the middle of the day?"

"They might," Maryam answers, sounding unsure.

"And wouldn't they haunt all year round, not just when we have a disco on?"

"Ah, but the first head teacher didn't like discos. I heard he had a bad experience on the dance floor when he was a kid – he had a whole routine and everything, but everyone laughed at him. So that's obviously why he's come back to stop our disco now, he hates them **THAT** much!" Maryam argues.

I shake my head. "I can't have this discussion right now, Maryam. I need to figure out who is doing this."

"It's the ghost!" Maryam insists.

"Yeah, okay, Maryam, maybe we'll chat to you later!" Mindy says brightly, moving me away.

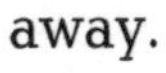

"She really believes it, doesn't she?" Manny says.

"A bit too much!" Milo adds.

"I've totally forgotten what I was saying before she came over," I say, shaking my head.

"You were saying how it could be someone from our year because all the incidents have happened when we've all been there."

"Plus the teachers," comments Milo, stroking Fang's head.

"The teachers?" I say. "Well, let's see. Miss Bunsen can't have done it – she was only in the science lab and not in the library or here. In fact, I remember her saying she was helping out with Year Three for the rest of the day because their normal teacher is off sick."

"Okay, so how about Mr Bound?" Mindy asks. "He was only at the library incident."

"Nah, he was way too freaked out after what happened in the library, you can't fake that," Manny says.

I think of something then. "You know who **WAS** at every incident?"

"Who?" Milo, Mindy and Manny ask me.

I nod towards Mr Graft. "Him."

"You can't be serious," Mindy says. "He wouldn't!"

"Well, we can't rule it out. He has been a bit over-the-top about all this Halloween stuff," I say.

"Yeah, but then he's shouting at everyone about the ghost trouble," Milo says. "Why would he do that if he's secretly the one sabotaging everything? Plus he almost got hit in the head with a book in the library so he couldn't have been the one throwing them!"

"That's a good point," I say. "Oh – but what if he's got an accomplice, someone helping him? And maybe all the shouting is just part of his plan to throw us off. Maybe he doesn't love Halloween at all and he's faking us out. Maybe he doesn't want the disco to go ahead? Grown-ups **ARE** weird. They have a different logic to kids," I say.

Mindy nods. "True!"

We watch Mr Graft walk across the room back to his ticket-selling table. He shouts something about making our way back to class once we've finished cleaning up. He pulls out a bag from under his table, which seems to be filled with brightly-coloured Halloween costumes, wigs and props. I can see a zombie hand and a plastic spider hanging out of the bag.

Manny shouts over. "Need a hand, sir? That bag looks heavy."

Mr Graft's eyes dart over to us. "**NO!**" he shouts and practically falls over the table as he tries to pack up his stuff and leave. He drops one of the wigs on the floor, so Manny runs over to pick it up for him.

"Cool wig, sir!" He grins, placing the big curly purple hairdo on his own head.

Mr Graft freaks out and snatches it away.

"These are not for children!" he snaps.

"That's not normal behaviour. Even for Mr Graft," I say as I watch.

"I think you're right, Neesh, definitely worth investigating," Milo says.

Manny comes over, looking a bit confused. "I was only trying to help!" He shrugs.

"Definitely dodgy," I say. "We need to keep an eye on him."

"I've just realized something," Milo says.

"What?" I ask, thinking it's something that could help us solve this mystery.

"We never even got to eat any lunch!" he exclaims, looking horrified.

CHAPTER SEVEN

SHOCKING SURPRISES!

After finding some cereal bars to keep us fuelled up, we get on with the rest of our day. Everywhere is full of whispering about the school being haunted. First I hear Davinder from the other Year Six class telling his friend he felt the ghost touch his shoulder earlier. Then Monika from our class says she heard that the ghost head teacher was actually a woman and she can't leave the school until she scares every child who walks through the door. Martin Miller from the year below gleefully tells anyone who will listen that the ghost head teacher is one of his ancestors and is going to take over the school and then the world!

It all gets more and more ridiculous with every new story I hear.

I kind of want to shout at them all that the whole haunting thing is daft and obviously fake, but we don't want whoever is pretending to be the ghost to realize we're on to them, so I stay quiet.

I think about Mr Graft some more. Could it really be him? Milo, Manny, Mindy and I agree to meet in the Year Three classroom round the corner from Mr Graft's office after last lesson, so we can see what he gets up to.

At home time, the school empties and soon it's just us. We're pretending to be working on a project in case anyone comes and asks why we're still here. Year Three have smaller chairs than us and they are so uncomfortable. I feel like a giant sitting on them! Manny keeps watch through the glass panel in the classroom door.

After about ten minutes we hear a door open.

"It's him!" Manny whispers, calling us over.

"He's leaving and he's got the bag of costumes with him!"

"We have to follow him, but we can't let him see us. Let's keep a bit of distance between us," I say.

Manny and Milo grin at each other. "Stealth mode!" they say in unison and then fist-bump.

Mindy sighs sarcastically. "Yay, here we go again."

"Right, focus, everyone!" I instruct. "This could be it."

We open the door carefully and quietly pad down the hallway after Mr Graft. He's whistling and swinging his giant bag, which looks like it's still filled with costumes and wigs. Something rolls out but he doesn't notice. When we get to it, I pick it up. It's a small tub of slime! That means it must be him, he's the ghost! And it looks like he's getting ready for his next trick! We need to follow him!

"He's not going to his car. Where is he walking to?" Mindy asks as we follow him outside.

He doesn't seem to notice us at all and marches off across the playground.

"That is odd. And he's taking the costumes with him," I say.

"I hope he's not going too far," Milo says. "It'll be dark soon!"

We wait for Mr Graft to get to the gate and then we run, quick as lightning, across the playground. When we reach the gate, he's already halfway down the street and crossing to the other side of the road. We soon see he's not going far at all as he heads into the community centre, which is less than two minutes' walk from our school.

We cross the road carefully and approach the community centre. Lively upbeat music is playing loudly from inside.

"We have to see in," I say.

We try to peer in the windows but they've got that one-way reflective glass that you can't see through. There's nothing else for it – we'll have to go in.

We push open the doors and walk into an entrance lobby. The music sounds even louder here, and I kind of recognize it. There's another set of solid wooden doors into the main hall, which is where the music is coming from. It sounds like salsa.*

"What now?" Milo asks.

"How are we going to see what's happening inside without giving ourselves away? Unless..." I say.

Mindy looks worried. "Unless?"

"Unless one of us climbs up on another's shoulders so they can see through that top panel of glass above the door."

"Isn't there something we can stand on?" Manny asks.

We look around but the lobby is empty except for a large whiteboard that says **CLOSED FOR**

***I only know about salsa music because of a disastrous day out with Aunty Bindi when she signed us up to a class. Salsa is a style of Latin American music and dance. It's very cool when you have rhythm, but let's just say that being co-ordinated is not exactly one of my strengths!**

PRIVATE EVENT. All the furniture is probably inside the main hall.

Milo steps forward. "I'll do it. Mindy, you're quite tall anyway, I bet if you stand on my shoulders you'll be able to see through that window no problem."

"Me? I don't know, Milo. I'm not great at balancing," Mindy says.

"We don't have a lot of time; Mr Graft could come out at any moment," I remind them.

Manny tries to reassure Mindy. "Look, sis, I'll help. We can be a pyramid. Put one foot on Milo and one on me and we'll be really stable, okay?"

Mindy doesn't look convinced but agrees. She hoists herself up onto the shoulders of Milo and Manny, who are both kneeling on the floor, but because Manny is slightly taller than Milo, she's a bit wonky. I reach up so she can hold onto my hand for support.

"Can you see anything?" I ask.

"Hmm, well..." Mindy starts as she peers through

the glass above the door. "I don't think Mr Graft is our fake ghost. Oh, that is just not pretty, I wish I hadn't seen that!"

"What is he doing in there?" Milo huffs. "Do you want to get down now? This is harder than I thought!"

"I'm not that heavy!" Mindy protests. "And yes, you can get me down."

But as Manny and Milo reach up to help Mindy, somehow they lose balance and tip forwards, then backwards. Before I can do anything to help, Mindy tumbles down, knocking me over as she does. I go flying into the board outside the doors with a loud

CRRRASH!

and we all land in a heap.

"Are you all okay?" I ask, picking myself up.

But they don't get a chance to answer, because the doors to the main hall burst open.

"What is going on out here?" Mr Graft shouts, before spotting us. His face changes then and his voice suddenly goes very high-pitched. "Oh, what are you children doing here?" he asks nervously, trying to pull the door closed so we can't see inside.

I try to peer into the hall but he moves to block my view.

"We...um...wanted to...erm—" But I can't think of anything!

"We know what you're doing in there!" Mindy shouts from the heap on the floor.

"We do?" I ask.

"We do!" Mindy grins.

"You do?" Mr Graft says, dismayed.

A face peers out at us from the gap between Mr Graft and the door frame.

"Who does?"

It's Granny Jas!

"Granny?" I say. "What are you doing here?"

"Ah, beta, you've ruined it!" Granny shrieks.

"Ruined what?" I ask, still clueless.

"**NOTHING!**" Mr Graft shouts, glaring at Granny. She glares right back at him.

"I know what! I saw it all," Mindy splutters. "They're doing a dance in there." She laughs, picking herself up from the ground. "Mr Graft is teaching them."

"Them?" I ask, my tummy doing a little turn.

"Our parents!" Mindy says, raising an eyebrow at Manny. "Yours too, Anisha."

"Mine?" I gulp. I don't like the sound of this at all!

"You might as well come in," sighs Mr Graft, moving out of the way.

We follow him into the hall. Mum's here and she's holding a feathered fan! Dad's here too, in a black shirt and trousers. Aunty Bindi is wearing a baggy top and leggings with some sparkly high heels. She's in the middle of a dance pose with Uncle Tony and gives us a little wave while Uncle Tony grimaces. "Hi, kids!"

I notice Miss Bunsen, Mr Bristles and even Miss File from the school office! They all wave sheepishly too. There are a few other parents here as well. Milo looks shocked as he spots his mum.

"What are you doing here, Mum? And why are you dancing with Poppy Simpson's dad!"

Milo's mum goes a bit pink in the face.

"What's actually going on?" I ask, not sure that I want to know or see more.

"We're learning salsa!" Aunty Bindi answers happily.

"It was meant to be a surprise." Granny Jas gives her a hard stare.

"Well, I know, but they're here now!" Bindi pouts.

"But why did you bring your big bag of costumes over here?" I ask Mr Graft. "And you dropped this jar of slime!"

"Well, it's not really any of your business but, if you must know, we are practising a spooky salsa and we were going to perform it at the school disco," Mr Graft admits. "And the slime was for my grandson. I don't get it but he loves the stuff!"

"Wow. Salsa. That is...um, great..." Mindy says.

"We're really quite good!" Granny beams.

"Can we see?" Milo asks.

"Oh, um, we don't have time," I stutter. I really don't want to see! "We should be going! Homework to do!"

"You'd rather do homework than watch our dance?" Dad smirks knowingly.

"I didn't say that!" I protest.

"That's okay, it'll be more fun if you see it on the night when we're all in costume." Mum smiles.

"But, why?" I ask. "Why would you want to perform at our school disco?"

"It was my idea actually," Mr Graft says. "When I was a young man, I was a ballroom-dancing champion. I won a medal at the North Birmingham Ballroom Finals for eleven-to-sixteen-year-olds!

Anyway, I've always loved dance, but I only learned salsa recently and it's so much fun! So I thought why should the disco only be for you children? I've been teaching some of the parents and teachers this special routine especially for the big night."

"Wow. Yeah, great idea," I say, even though it's not great at all.

"Come on, Anni, you can join in too. Look, it's just shaking your hips, it's easy," Aunty Bindi says, giving me a demonstration.

I glance at Mindy and Manny, who are obviously as horrified as I am, and I say, "That's okay, we really do have studying to do. See you at home later!"

We all run out of there faster than we've ever run before.

So much for catching the fake ghost. We got much more than we expected or wanted. Sometimes investigating has its downsides!

CHAPTER EIGHT

THE CLOCK IS TICKING!

After cringing most of the night with thoughts of my family dancing salsa at our spooky disco, I wake up late for school and have to rush to get ready.

Granny is in the kitchen, looking very grumpy.

"Everything okay, Granny?" I ask. "Is it the house move? I've been meaning to ask you how things are going. There must be something we can do to stop it?"

"Well, I'm trying, **beta**, but my original plan didn't quite work out. Can you believe your parents thought I was being helpful by packing up the kitchen equipment and they started joining in?

They said they were very glad I had obviously changed my mind and it showed them they were making the right decision. Totally wrong! So, I've realized I have to switch to a harder tactic. That was too much mind-messing. I have to be **DIRECT** so there is no confusion!"

"What does that mean?" I ask, slightly worried.

"I'm going on strike," she says proudly, holding up a sign that says *GRANNIES HAVE RIGHTS TOO!* She turns it round and on the other side it says, *I will NOT be moved!*

"Wow!" I say. "Have Mum and Dad seen this yet?"

"No, but they will, beta, they will!" she replies.

"I, um, I'm not sure it's the best way to get them to rethink the house move, Granny," I say.

"I am! They need to know they can't push me around. I may be old but I will not be forced to move out of my home! I have rights, I will be heard!"

"Okay, well do me a favour, Granny, and just try to stay calm. It's not good for you to get upset," I say.

"I'm calm, beta. I am taking a stand, that's all," Granny replies, standing boldly with her sign.

I kiss her on the cheek and leave for school. This has got to be the most stressful week in the history of my life. My granny is on strike. My parents are selling our house. My school is being haunted by a fake ghost.

I meet Milo down the road. "Woah, Neesh, are you alright? You're all messy and not like your normal neat self. What happened?" he asks.

"Rough night!" I say. "I had weird dreams about the spooky disco. Skeleton Fred and Ghastly

Gertrude were there too! Everyone was salsa dancing and I was on stage dressed as a pumpkin, but I had a cold and I kept sneezing out slime! It was really gross!"

"Cool! I can never remember my dreams," Milo moans.

"To top it all, I woke up to find my granny has gone on strike! She thinks it will help convince my parents not to sell the house," I explain. "I feel like it's just going to make things worse. This week just gets weirder and weirder. Come on, we'd better get to school. We're back to where we started after we discovered it's not Mr Graft trying to ruin the disco, so we need to come up with a new suspect."

When we get there, the school is all abuzz with

rumours of the ghost and people talking about what happened at lunch yesterday – except the story changes depending on who's telling it. I'm sure I overhear someone saying Mr Graft chopped the head off a five-headed slime monster! A boy runs past us from the toilets with a sheet over his head. He's chasing his friend and making "**WOOOOOOOO!**" sounds. The whole school seems to have gone wild.

As we go past the school office, I hear the receptionist complaining that Skeleton Fred had been left in her chair and gave her a right fright this morning. He's still there, propped up in an empty chair to one side, and Milo gives him a little wave. Then someone says Ghastly Gertrude is floating in the Year Four boys' toilets, but it turns out that one of the boys has draped a load of toilet paper by the vent and the air is making it move. All the boys in Year Four get a good telling-off for that from Mr Helix. I feel bad for the kids who didn't do anything.

After registration Mr Helix announces that we can go to the library to change our books. I'm so happy – finally, some good news!

When we reach the library, Mr Bound is waiting for us.

"Hi, children, let me just get the door unlocked," he says cheerfully. "Oh, that's strange, I could have sworn I locked this door yesterday when I left." As he opens the door and switches on the lights, he stops suddenly. We all slowly step inside to see what has Mr Bound shaking and pointing.

It's Fred the skeleton! He's sitting on a beanbag in the middle of the floor surrounded by books.

They're all scary books too, by the looks of it.

"Wait, we just saw Fred in the school office, how did he get here?" I say.

Mr Bound screeches, "**Who did it?** Come on, own up! Someone is messing with my library and I won't have it – I won't have it, I tell you!" he mutters to himself.

"What on earth has happened?" Mr Helix says, coming up behind us.

"That skeleton, Frank, or whatever his name is! I was keeping watch all afternoon yesterday and nothing remotely spooky happened. But we've just come in this morning and he's there!"

I glance over at Mindy and Manny, who look just as weirded out as everyone else. Milo isn't fazed at all of course.

"What book do you think Fred is reading?" he asks me.

"Um, I don't think skeletons can read, Milo," I say. "I'm more interested in how Fred got from the school office to the library in such a short amount of time. I doubt he just wandered over here by himself!"

Mr Bound starts herding us out of the library. "You'll have to come back tomorrow, children. I'm closing the library for the day again," he says. "My nerves have had enough shock for one day."

"You can't just give in," I say.

"Sorry, Anisha. Hopefully Mr Graft can get a handle on who or what is behind it all, otherwise, at this rate, the disco will have to be cancelled," Mr Helix says, shrugging apologetically. "It's out of our hands if the governors get involved."

"We can't let that happen, Neesh!" Milo pleads as Mr Helix and Mr Bound leave us outside the library, which is once again all locked up.

Milo's right. "Okay, let's go and see Mr Graft," I decide. "We have to get him on side. Buy ourselves some time to investigate a bit more before they make any decisions about the disco."

We walk round to Mr Graft's office. His door is slightly ajar but he's on the phone, so we wait outside. It sounds like he's talking to someone really important.

"Yes, I do appreciate we need to make a decision. None of us wants to see the disco get cancelled. Yes, of course. Okay, I'll be in touch." He hangs up the phone with a sigh. Yeesh, maybe this isn't a great time to talk to him! But it's too late, Milo has already knocked on the door and suddenly we're going in.

"Anisha, Milo. What can I do for you?" he asks. "Is it about the salsa dancing?"

"Well, sir, it's more what we can do for you," I say.

Mr Graft stifles a smile. "Oh really? And what is it you think I need right now?"

"I'd say you need this fake ghost to be exposed so the Halloween disco can go ahead," I answer, with Milo nodding enthusiastically next to me.

"Well, yes, that would help. We can't have everyone too scared to go, it'll be a complete flop."

"Not if we uncover who's causing trouble!" Milo pipes up. "We found evidence in the library yesterday!" He explains about the catapult.

"Oh, you did? Running your own little investigation, are you? Why didn't you come to me yesterday then?" Mr Graft asks.

I blush. "Um, because we kind of thought it might be you..."

Mr Graft laughs then, a full-on belly laugh. "Me? Why on earth? I **LOVE** Halloween! Why would I try to ruin it? That's actually cheered me up, children!"

He laughs for a moment more and then straightens up. "Okay, so you've ruled me out, who else is in the frame? I know you, Anisha Mistry, you're good at mystery-solving. Who are your suspects?"

"That's what we're stuck on," I admit. "We're trying to think of who would want to do all this and what they would gain from it."

"Maybe it's someone who hates Halloween?" Milo suggests.

"I don't love it, but I wouldn't go to all this trouble to wreck it," I point out.

"Okay, someone who really doesn't want the disco to go ahead, for whatever reason," Mr Graft says.

"You know who recently said they were scared of the disco and didn't think it was a good idea for it to go ahead?" I speak slowly as a thought forms in my mind.

Milo and I look at each other. "Maryam!"

"Maryam Afzal?" Mr Graft says incredulously. "Never! She's such a quiet girl."

"That doesn't mean she couldn't do it, sir," I say.

"She has been acting a bit weird about all the disco stuff and she was totally freaking out at lunch yesterday," Milo says.

"Ah, she was, wasn't she!" I remember. "Maybe she thinks if she can stop the disco going ahead then nothing bad will happen. Although she's kind of the one making *actual* bad stuff happen!"

"But what evidence do you have?" asks Mr Graft.

"Well...all we have so far is the catapult from the library and a hunch. None of that ties Maryam to the ghost for sure. Let us investigate a bit more first and then, if we find anything out, we'll come straight to you," I say.

Mr Graft frowns, which makes his eyebrows knit together. "Yes, we don't want to accuse anyone unfairly. And actually, now I think about it, Maryam's mother is on the board of governors, so yes, let's tread carefully – we don't want to attract any unnecessary attention to everything that's going on!"

We agree that Milo and I will try and suss out Maryam this afternoon and report back later. In the meantime, Mr Graft says he'll be researching ways to banish ghosts. Just in case we're wrong and it is a real one!

We decide it would be a good idea to check out Fang's tank for any clues too, in case someone did let him out on purpose yesterday. We drop by the lab on the way back to class. Thankfully no one is using it at the moment and Miss Bunsen is nowhere to be seen. Milo starts cooing over Fang straight away.

"Hello, beautiful boy, how are you?" he says, gently taking Fang out of his tank.

"Now," I say, "let's see what's in here. Whoever let him out might have left a clue behind."

I peer into the tank from above. There's Fang's log that he slithers around. Some dried leaves and rocks. I carefully move some of the leaves aside with the end of a pencil. That's when I see it. A thin flash of orange tangled up in the branch of Fang's spiky plant in the corner of the tank. I pull it out carefully and show it to Milo, who is now

blowing kisses at Fang. "Milo, look! Another orange hair like the one we found on the catapult in the library. Our fake ghost was definitely here – we just need to prove who it was now! Someone with orange hair? Or wearing an orange wig."

Milo turns back to Fang and places him back in the tank. "Don't worry, Fang, we'll find out who's been using you to cause chaos," he promises.

After lunch, everyone's got some free time to do more disco prep – even though half the class are whispering about not going since all these weird things have been happening. Our whole year group is in the hall together, so it's the perfect opportunity to approach Maryam. All the teachers are there too, organizing small groups of us for different activities.

One group is making streamers, another a backdrop for photos, and another group is making spooky masks. I think to myself that it could all end up being for nothing if the fake ghost gets their way. I won't get a last celebration with my friends before my parents make me move away. This is all just so rubbish, it can't end like that. It just can't.

Mindy and Manny end up in the group making masks. Milo and I join Maryam's group, which also unfortunately has Beena Bhatt in it, but we have to do it for the sake of the disco. It's just the four of us, so hopefully it will be easy to ask our questions. We're unravelling some long strings of lights and testing each set are working. Milo partners with Beena reluctantly and she immediately starts telling him off for not doing it right. I don't think they've even begun yet!

I turn to Maryam, who is quietly unwrapping a set of lights.

"Hey, Maryam, how are you?" I ask.

"Oh, um, okay," she answers.

"I guess this isn't your idea of fun," I say. "You don't like Halloween much, do you?"

"No, I hate it – but I suppose it's better than maths!" Maryam jokes.

"Ha, yeah," I say, even though I actually really like maths.

"It was wild what happened at lunch yesterday with the slime in the canteen, wasn't it? This ghost is really trying to scare us all," Maryam comments, not looking up from the tangle of wires in her hand.

"Well, I don't think it's a real ghost," I say.

"You don't?" Maryam asks, looking surprised. "Even after the flying books in the library? Then the slime in the canteen and the –" she shudders – "ugh...snake! Skeleton Fred keeps moving around the school by himself too. How can that not be supernatural?"

I don't know why, but I decide in that moment I'm just going to ask her outright. "Yeah, but a real person could have done all that," I say. "Someone who maybe doesn't like Halloween or scary stuff. You know, like...you?"

Maryam looks up at me then. "What? You think... **ME?**"

Beena and Milo look over at us. I just grin back, like. *Nothing to see here!* Beena glares and returns to lecturing Milo about how to untangle the lights properly. Poor Milo!

I look at Maryam. "Come on, you've got to admit you'd be the perfect suspect. You spent all that time trying to convince us there's a ghost – in fact, you're the one who started all the stories about the head teacher ghost. You hate the idea of a Halloween disco so it would be ideal for you if it got cancelled. You could have somehow rigged Skeleton Fred, planted the slime and let Fang out of his tank," I say.

Maryam laughs. "I didn't start the stories, I just repeated what my sister told me. And of course it's not me! If you haven't noticed, I'm scared of **EVERYTHING**! I can't even imagine trying to scare other people. Plus, I hate slime. And as for the snake – getting it out of its tank and holding it? Urgh, that rubbery cold skin!" She shudders. "Oh, I just couldn't, I couldn't! Milo even had to take it away from me yesterday, so how could I have been the one who let it out?"

I think for a second, remembering how she reacted around Fang. She's got a point. It wouldn't make much sense for it to be her. Oh! My tummy dips as I realize that I think Maryam is telling the truth. "Okay, you're right. I'm sorry for accusing you. But if it wasn't you, and we have evidence it's not an actual ghost, who else could it be?" I ask.

Maryam shrugs. "I don't know, but they must be very organized to have set all this up. Some of the stuff that's happened is similar to the stories my sister told me, but this ghost seems to have upgraded their methods. The flying books are new and so is Skeleton Fred moving around."

"Do you remember anything else your sister told you about the original haunting? Maybe there's something in that which might help us," I say.

Maryam thinks for a moment. "Nothing more than what I told you," she says eventually. "You could try talking to Beena, though, she was one of the first people I talked to about it and she seemed to already know about it."

Just then there's a commotion at the other end of

the hall. Somebody screams. A few kids run from the corner of the room towards us. A gap opens up in the crowd and I see one of the girls is wearing Fang round her neck

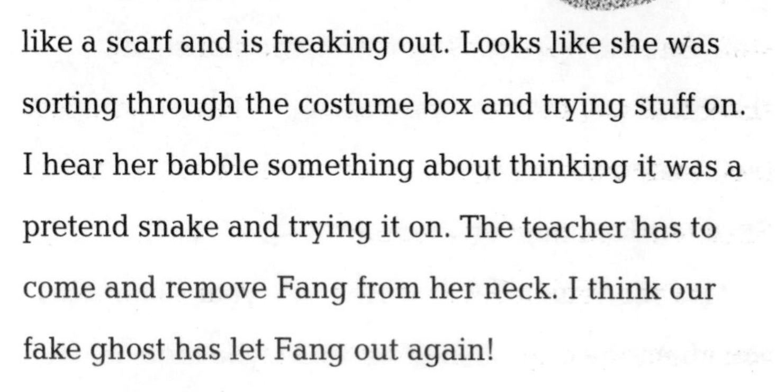

like a scarf and is freaking out. Looks like she was sorting through the costume box and trying stuff on. I hear her babble something about thinking it was a pretend snake and trying it on. The teacher has to come and remove Fang from her neck. I think our fake ghost has let Fang out again!

Maryam shivers next to me. "Ugh, I can't look at it, it's just too...ugh."

She continues to make *ick* noises until Beena says, "For goodness' sake, Maryam, get a grip, it's just a snake! He's probably more frightened of us than we are of him. He's actually quite docile when you hold him."

"I didn't know you liked animals, Beena." Milo raises an eyebrow. "Maybe Fang doesn't like his tank much. I might talk to Miss Bunsen about setting him free. Would you like to come too?"

Beena looks at Milo with disgust. "Er...obviously not. Don't think you know me because I made one comment about a snake."

"Alright, no need to be rude to him, Beena! No wonder no one wants to come to your party," Maryam says suddenly.

I think Beena might say something really nasty back, but she doesn't. She just turns away from us and keeps unwinding her string of lights in silence.

Milo smiles gratefully at Maryam for sticking up for him, but I can't stop thinking about how sad and small Beena looks.

At the end of the lesson I report back to Mr Graft about Maryam. We agree I'll keep investigating but it's feeling more and more like the fake ghost is winning. Will we ever figure this mystery out?

CHAPTER NINE

GRANNY ON STRIKE!

Later on, when Mindy, Manny, Milo and I get back to my house, it's chaos. Granny Jas has stuck to her word and fully gone on strike. She is refusing to cook until my parents "stop their foolishness" about moving house. She's still holding her sign, which I can tell is really annoying my parents but they're trying not to show it. Mum is making dinner instead, but feeling under pressure with Granny glaring at her. She's spilled turmeric all over the counter, got the garam masala and the chilli powder measurements mixed up and left the hob on too high, so the spices have burned. The smell in the kitchen grabs me by the throat, making me cough.

"Takeaway anyone?" Dad smiles tightly.

"Pizza?" Manny asks hopefully.

"How long is Granny on strike for?" Aunty Bindi complains. "I miss her cooking."

"It's only been one day, sweetums," Uncle Tony tries to point out, but Bindi gives him a look.

Granny smiles sweetly. "As long as it takes."

"Now listen here, Mum..." Dad starts, but shrinks back a little when Granny stares at him.

Mindy, Manny and I all look at each other. "Shall we go upstairs and chill till the food arrives?" I ask.

"Good idea," Mindy replies.

"Wow, things are super tense in your house," Manny comments as we go into my room. "Granny's not messing about, is she?"

"I know, I'm just hoping it works," I agree. "Okay, let's write down what we know about the fake ghost." I grab my notepad off my bedside table and flick to a new page.

Incidents:

- **Science lab – Lights flickering, board comes on and Fred moves by himself**
- **Library – Books flying, catapult, orange hair**
- **Canteen – Slime instead of soup, Fang out of his tank**
- **Library – Skeleton Fred posed with scary books**
- **Hall – Fang getting into the costume box**

"I wish Fang could have a bigger tank or a more natural habitat," Milo interrupts. "I don't think he likes his tank. I wouldn't like to be stuck in a glass box, would you? I've been seriously thinking I should talk to Miss Bunsen about it."

"It's no different to you keeping Larry the lobster in a tank," Mindy points out.

Milo puffs out his chest. "I **SAVED** Larry from a cruel cooking-pot fate!" he declares.

"Okay, let's not get distracted," I say, tapping the notepad. "Right, what else do we know?"

I make a note:

What do these incidents have in common?

- **Catapult and orange hair found in library suggests it is a person doing these things and not a ghost!**
- **Orange hair found in Fang's tank as well**

Suspects:

- ~~Mr Graft~~
- ~~Maryam~~
- ?

- **Someone who knows about the ghost legend and is using it to scare everyone!**
- **Somebody who isn't afraid of snakes**
- **Somebody with orange hair**

Motive:

To stop the disco – but why? They don't like discos?

I stop writing and look at the page. I've written, *Somebody with orange hair*. I look up at Milo.

I think about the orange hair we found. It is a very similar colour to Milo's. Could it be…?

No, Milo would never… Would he?

Milo is excited for the disco, why would he try to ruin it?

BUT he did just say again how Fang shouldn't be kept cooped up. Maybe he thinks he was doing a good thing?

I can't suspect my best friend though. No, this is silly. I should just ask him.

"Hey, Milo, you know when you said before about how Fang shouldn't be in that small tank – you wouldn't deliberately let him loose though, right?" I ask.

"What? No! That would be dangerous for Fang. The school is full of kids, he could get stomped on!" Milo says, horrified. "Is everything okay, Neesh? You look a bit distressed."

Mindy looks at me then. "Why did you ask him that?"

"I was just wondering, that's all," I lie.

Mindy frowns. "You couldn't think Milo is behind all this? Milo isn't the fake ghost, silly!"

My face feels hot. "I know, I know, I'm sorry. This mystery is just getting to me."

Milo studies my face. "And you thought it was me? Anisha, how long have we been friends?"

"For ever," I say. "I'm sorry, I knew it wouldn't be you. I was just thinking about the orange hair, and then you said that thing about Fang, and I didn't really, truly think it was you but...you know...I just got a bit carried away there."

Milo laughs – a big belly laugh. "Can you imagine? Me? The suspect? That would really be a surprise, wouldn't it?"

Manny cackles. "Milo, the fake ghost – that's too funny!"

"It's not that funny," I say, a bit annoyed that I even let my mind go there for a second.

"It kind of is, Neesh. Anyway, I can't be the only person in the world with orange hair," says Milo.

"Maybe not the world, but you're the only one in the school with **BRIGHT** orange hair," I say.

"Actually, I'm not," Milo says.

"You're not?"

"No, what about the new kid? She joined our class this term – but she's been off sick for a couple of days, remember? Ruby."

I press my face into the palm of my hand. I can't believe I forgot. The new kid! She has orange hair too. But why would she want to ruin the disco? She barely knows us all and she's hardly been here to do anything anyway!

When the pizza arrives, we go back downstairs. Aunty Bindi convinces Granny to sit with us and eat.

"So, kids, what's been happening at school? How are the preparations for the Halloween disco coming along?" Uncle Tony asks us.

"Well, someone's trying to ruin it and make everyone think the school is haunted, but apart from that, cool," Mindy answers.

"Oh, um, right," Uncle Tony replies, looking confused.

"But the disco won't be cancelled or anything, will it? I've bought a dress for our performance and it's very sparkly." Aunty Bindi beams.

"We don't know. But I think we have a new suspect to look into tomorrow," I say, as I bite into a large slice of cheesy pizza – my favourite! "But, you know, maybe your performance would be better another time? You could have more time to rehearse and do it next year instead?"

Aunty Bindi considers this and then realizes something. "But, Anni, you're in Year Six now so you won't be in that school next year!"

"Exactly!" snorts Mindy. "We won't have to watch it then!"

"Harsh!" Uncle Tony says. "But I understand. I guess I wouldn't have wanted to watch my mum and dad dance around in front of my whole school either."

Aunty Bindi giggles. "I suppose. But we are very good, I promise. You're going to love it! And it might be the last time we get to do something like this for a while."

"What do you mean, last time?" I ask, thinking she means the house move which still makes my tummy turn. If Mum and Dad get their way I won't be here in the next few months, never mind next year!

Aunty Bindi smiles widely at Uncle Tony. "We wanted to talk to you all about something, it's **SO** exciting—"

But before she can say anything more, the phone rings.

Dad answers it, and he mouths to Mum that it's the estate agent. They take the phone into another room.

Granny huffs, flings her sign to one side and then turns to me. "My hard bowling tactics are not working, beta. Time for phase three and something a bit more emotional." And with that she leaves the table and goes off to her room.

"All the grown-ups in this family are weird," Manny announces, chomping on another slice of pizza.

"I wonder what Bindi was going to tell us?" Mindy murmurs as Bindi and Tony go off into the kitchen.

"I feel like it can wait," I say. "We have enough going on already. I don't want any more surprises till we've dealt with the disco and the fake ghost. Tomorrow we investigate the new kid – Ruby!"

CHAPTER TEN

PUMPKIN PYRAMID

We never get to finish the conversation with our family and by the next morning I'm worrying about what's going on at school again. We're decorating pumpkins today, which sounds kind of fun – as long as nothing else goes wrong…

But first I need to check out Ruby. Luckily, we have assembly first thing. As our year group piles into the hall, I see her. She's two rows behind me. I haven't seen her around much before. I guess us four just stick together a lot, so I don't often notice other kids. Plus, like Milo said, she's been off sick. I think that's why I forgot about her.

She turns and sees me staring and smiles at me. I smile back nervously. I still have the hair from the library. If I could somehow get one of Ruby's hairs, I could compare the two.

As I'm looking at her again, a noise at the back of the hall makes her look round and I see something that gives me an idea. Her scrunchie! I cough and nod at Mindy, who is in the row behind me, the one in front of Ruby. I point at my hair, pulling it back in a small ponytail and then I point towards Ruby.

Mindy nods back like she understands. Luckily people are still chatting as the last class walks in and gets settled. Mindy turns quickly and says she likes Ruby's scrunchie, can she see it? Ruby looks confused but takes it out and shows it to her. As quick as lightning, I see Mindy grab a stray hair that is caught in the scrunchie before passing it back to Ruby. Phew, we got it.

As we walk back to class after assembly, Mindy, Manny, Milo and I hang at the back of the line.

"You got it!" I say. "My tummy was doing somersaults. I wasn't sure you'd understood what I was trying to signal."

"I think Ruby thought you were being weird about her scrunchie," Manny adds.

Mindy laughs. "Well, it worked, didn't it?"

I pull out the hair we found in the library and Mindy pulls out the one from Ruby's scrunchie. This is it. The moment of orange truth.

Except it isn't.

It isn't a match.

"Wait, they're not the same colour!" Milo cries.

"The one from Ruby is darker." Mindy groans.

"So it isn't her?" Manny asks.

"No," I moan. "It doesn't look like it."

I can't believe this. We got it wrong *again*. Now what? We're back to where we started!

But there's no more time to chat because we have to get to maths.

Beena annoys everyone right from the start of the lesson by asking to make an announcement and then listing ten reasons why her party is going to be the event of the year. She just does not give up! Her reasons are:

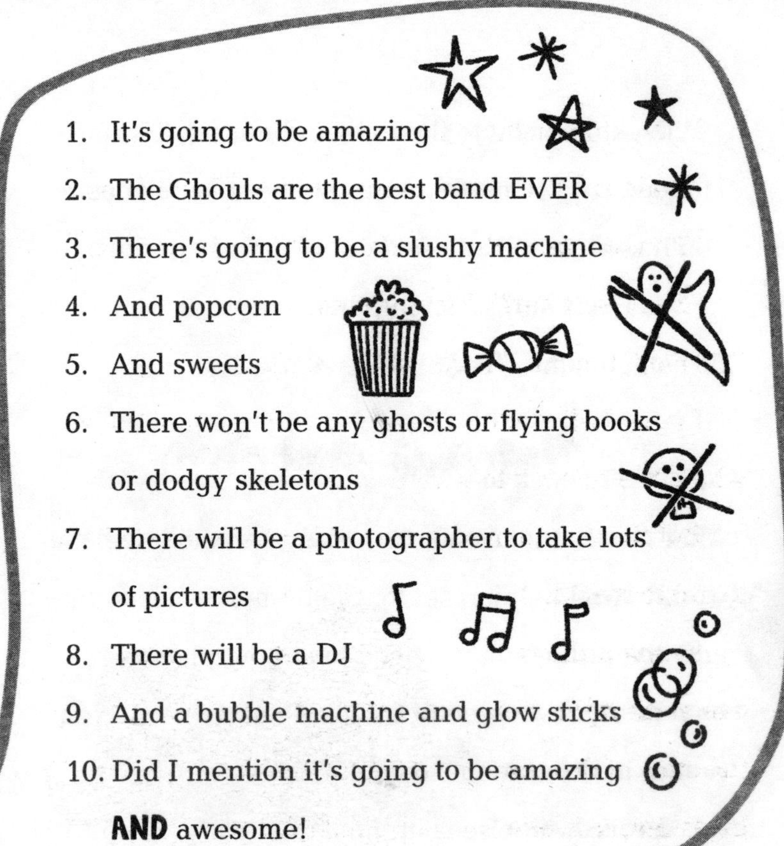

She doesn't just read the points out either. She describes each one and why it's going to be so cool. We're all falling asleep by the time she's done! Someone makes the mistake of saying that if they can wear their Frankenstein costume then they'll come and Beena loses it.

She stomps off to the toilets, shouting, "Stupid Halloween! My party is going to be so much cooler, you'll see – you'll all see!"

Mr Helix sighs. "Right, that went well. Shall we do some maths, Year Six?"

After break, Mr Graft asks Mindy and me if we would mind helping set up the pumpkin-decorating activity in the hall. We need to get out plenty of benches for everyone to sit on. He gives us a box of pumpkin decorations to take with us.

"Everything else is in the hall already. I had Mr Bristles leave the big boxes of pumpkins in there this morning. Just set them out, one per place-setting, along with the stickers and marker pens. I would have liked us to carve some as well, but sharp tools in school are definitely a safety issue, so we'll have to settle for decorating them instead."

"Okay, sir," I say. "Does this mean the disco

is definitely going ahead?"

"Well, as long as we don't have any more frightful incidents," Mr Graft says, raising an eyebrow. "I've had a very uncomfortable conversation with the head of the board of governors this morning and if we have one more, they want us to cancel the disco. There can't be any further trouble. Not after the last time – it's taken the school a long time to recover from what happened."

"Was it really that bad, sir?" Mindy asks.

Mr Graft frowns. "Whatever you've heard, it was worse! Everyone was so jittery around here after the last disco. The governors wouldn't come in and when they did they insisted on sending in someone to check for anything spooky first! And for years I had to answer questions about whether the school really was haunted. We even made it into the local paper because of it. Parents were afraid to send their children here! They actually believed there was a ghost! We can't have all that again. We have to keep things running smoothly and very much **NOT** haunted!"

"I'm sure it will be okay, sir!" I say cheerfully, although in my head I'm not convinced.

Mr Graft gets called away then, so Mindy and I make our way to the hall to start setting up for the pumpkin-decorating.

We're chatting about what we're going to put on our own pumpkins when we walk in and— Oh no!

The pumpkins are NOT in the box like Mr Graft had said they would be. They're on the floor. Stacked in a giant pyramid shape. They are all facing us and someone has written across them in marker pen the words *NO DISCO!* in huge letters!

"Woah!" Mindy shouts.

We stand there in silence for a moment, just staring. The ghost has struck again!

"Mr Graft is going to freak," I say, looking more closely. "We can't let him see this. I think the marker should wipe off, so we can still decorate the pumpkins as planned. Whoever did this probably just wanted to scare everyone when they came in – but they didn't count on Mr Graft asking us to get here beforehand."

Just then there's a noise from behind the pumpkin pyramid and I see movement.

"Hey, is someone there?" I shout. There's a pounding in my chest. Could it be the person behind all this? Am I finally going to catch them?

There is no answer, so I move closer. There's a thump as one pumpkin hits the floor. I step back and so does Mindy, before suddenly the pyramid of pumpkins gives way and pumpkins are rolling everywhere! I grab onto Mindy as pumpkins come at us from every angle. One ends up under my feet and I'm trying to stay upright but it's rolling and I'm wobbling all over the place!

Just then I hear the sound of footsteps running away. Someone must have been hiding behind the pyramid and pushed it so it fell over! I finally manage to get onto solid ground where it's safe and see a figure escape through the double doors which lead out onto the playground. I can't tell who it is

because they're wearing a hoodie, but it's definitely a kid. Then they trip and stumble forwards so their hood falls back a bit. I still don't see their face because they have their back to me, but I do see a flash of orange hair! They pick themselves up and run at breakneck speed across the playground, vanishing round the corner.

"Did you see that?" I yell to Mindy, who is still picking herself up.

"No, who was it?"

"I don't know," I say. "But they definitely had orange hair!"

"But we already know it's not Milo or Ruby! Who could it be?" asks Mindy.

"I'm not sure yet but I know I can solve this mystery; I just need a bit longer," I reply.

"We're running out of time though, Anisha. The disco is tomorrow. We have to start putting up decorations in the morning!" Mindy points out.

I think for a second. "Every single time we're about to do some disco prep, the 'ghost' does something to freak everyone out," I say. "First when we were making decorations in the science lab, then in the library at the disco-planning meeting. Later when Mr Graft was selling disco tickets and then again when we were going to decorate pumpkins. There's a pattern to our fake ghost's sabotage."

"Yeah, good thinking. But how does that help us find out who they are?" Mindy asks.

"Well, if my theory is true, they are sure to try and stop us somehow when we put up decorations tomorrow," I say. "I think it's time we set a trap!"

CHAPTER ELEVEN

CANCELLED?

We don't have long to gather up and wipe down the pumpkins plus lay them all out neatly before the rest of our class arrive to decorate them. No one seems to notice anything is wrong though, so it looks like we covered up the latest fake ghost attack successfully. Mr Helix is supervising everyone while decorating his own pumpkin, which he seems really excited about. He's got stick-on googly eyes and he's made some hair out of lime-green wool. Everyone settles down quite quickly, so Mindy and I go to sit down near Milo and Manny. We tell them what happened and how the person running away definitely had orange hair.

Milo scratches his head. "Did you ever think it could be a wig? There are so many wigs and costumes around the school at the moment. Maybe the culprit picked up one of those to disguise themselves?" he suggests.

"That DOES make sense." Mindy nods.

I blush. "You're right. I'm sorry I even slightly thought it could have been you yesterday, Milo," I say.

Milo shrugs. "It's okay, I do have a very unique and special look. Although, this person is giving us orange-haired people a bad reputation which makes me want to catch them even more!"

"Agreed," I say.

Just then there's a commotion at the front of the hall. Mr Graft is speaking quite urgently with a woman I don't recognize. Maryam is sitting behind us and shouts out, "Mum?"

Oh no! It's Maryam's mum – and she's a school governor!

She comes over to Maryam. "Don't worry, darling," she says. "I'm just explaining to Mr Graft that the disco needs to be cancelled."

Mr Graft is very red in the face and his left eye is twitching.

"There's no cause for alarm, Mrs Afzal. As I've explained, we have everything under control.

Look, the children are decorating the pumpkins beautifully!"

"Why is your eye twitching?" Maryam's mum asks.

"Oh…it's, um…an infection," Mr Graft lies.

"It's twitching again! I think you are fibbing to me, Mr Graft!" Maryam's mum says sternly.

Mr Graft laughs nervously. "No, no, we just have a lot going on in school – but as I said, no cause for worry."

"That's not what Maryam has been telling me, Mr Graft," Mrs Afzal says.

Everyone looks at Maryam, who hides her face behind her hands.

"I…I didn't think you'd come to school, Mum!" Maryam moans behind her hands.

"Well, sweetheart, the governors were already concerned about this disco and it seems rightly so! Mr Graft, what is this I hear about skeletons roaming the halls and flying books in the library?" she accuses.

Mr Graft looks like he wants to run away. "Well, yes, we've had some issues, but I can assure you—"

"No!" Mrs Afzal cuts him off. "You listen to me! One more incident and Halloween is done in this school **for good**!"

Mr Graft sees us all watching and shouts, "Back to what you were doing, children, this is not your concern!"

Everyone pretends to carry on decorating their pumpkins, but we're all still secretly listening. Mr Graft tries to steer Mrs Afzal towards the doors, but she's not having any of it. She starts going round some of the tables and talking to the children, asking them what they know about the so-called ghost.

Unfortunately, the first table she goes to has

Beena on it, who, of course, is delighted to tell her how terribly things have been going. I can hear her annoying voice. "Oh yes, Mrs Afzal, I think Maryam was right to come to you. It has been a shambles, honestly! I tried to encourage everyone to forget about the school disco, but you know children once they're fixed on an idea."

"Isn't she a child too?" Milo comments.

"You wouldn't think so the way she's talking. She's loving this. I notice she's not mentioning how she's been in a strop about the disco being on the same day as her birthday party," I say.

Beena continues, "I mean the slime alone was a health hazard! Imagine if a child had eaten some by mistake!"

Mrs Afzal looks horrified then. "**SLIME!** What slime? I didn't know about any slime!" she shouts hysterically. "If the newspapers ever found out about it, we'd be in so much trouble. What about health and safety? The school could be shut down!"

Everyone gasps. Have the school shut down? I know I might be moving, but I can see the worry on my friend's faces. I can't let that happen. It's bad enough if I have to leave but I can't imagine the school not being here at all and **EVERYONE** having to leave!

Beena goes a bit pink in the cheeks. "Really? I never thought about that. They wouldn't really close the school, would they? The school couldn't really be shut down?" She stops then and looks around. "You know, I feel a bit ill. I think I need to go to the toilet. Is that okay, sir?" she asks Mr Graft.

Mr Graft glares at Beena but steps aside and says, "Yes, just go." He turns to Mrs Afzal. "Lovely girl, bit dramatic at times!"

Mrs Afzal nods and moves on. After hearing that, everyone else she speaks to makes sure to play down how much has been going on in school. Mrs Afzal frowns but seems to buy it. She has a word with Maryam before she leaves and then lets a relieved Mr Graft escort her out.

"Right, back to it, Year Six," Mr Helix says. "I think that's enough excitement for one lesson."

We carry on with our pumpkins, but my mind is whirring with everything that's been happening. I see Beena re-enter the hall, but then she tells the teacher she doesn't feel well and she goes home for the rest of the day. It's so weird. One minute she was gleefully telling Mrs Afzal how haunted the school is and the next she looked like she was going to be sick! That is dodgy!

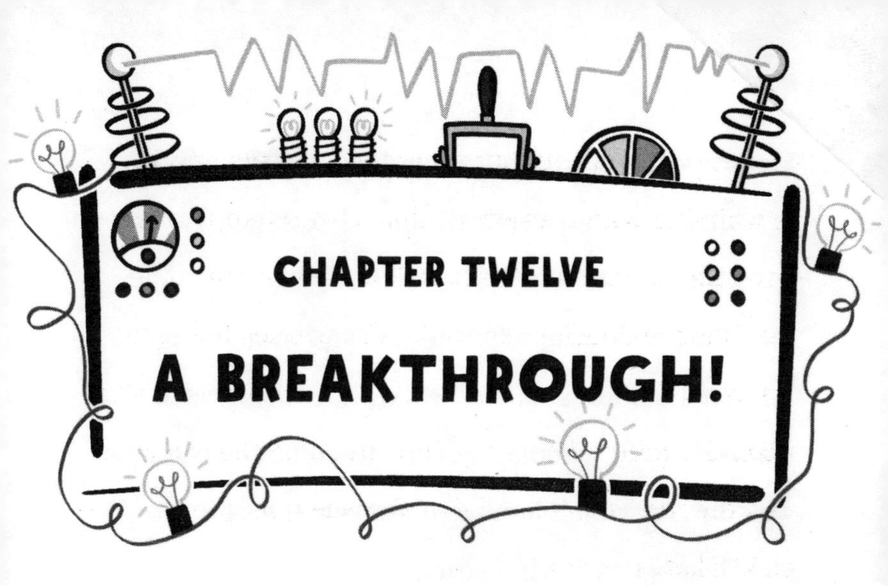

CHAPTER TWELVE

A BREAKTHROUGH!

All the way home, I can't stop thinking about what Beena said and how she reacted when Mrs Afzal said the school could be closed down. I play all the things that have happened in the past week over in my mind. I'm hoping Milo doesn't notice I'm only half-listening to him talking about the Spookbuster costumes his nan's made.

"And the buttons glow in the dark, Neesh!" he says excitedly. "Neesh, are you listening to me? What did I just say?"

"Buttons?" I say.

"What's going on? You've been quiet since the

pumpkin decorating. Is it the disco stuff?"

"Just thinking about Beena," I explain.

Milo pulls a face. "Oh, why?"

"I'm wondering why she was so eager to tell Maryam's mum about all the stuff that's been happening at school. She's not the type of person you'd think would believe in ghosts. It's weird."

"That's true," Milo agrees.

"And I know Beena is a pain and we just ignore her a lot of the time but, if you think about it, she's the perfect suspect for this. She wants her party to be a success, right? But no one wants to go to her party while the disco is happening, which is why she hates the disco and has been moaning about it every chance she gets. So, if the disco got cancelled that would solve all her problems."

"Yeah, but there's still no guarantee people would come to her party – she's so mean to everyone," Milo points out.

"I'm not sure that's how Beena thinks things

work, Milo." I sigh. "I mean, it's just a thought, but I feel like there's something in it. She could be the one?"

"Maybe. But how do we prove it? Plus, would she really go to all that trouble? She doesn't usually like to do anything herself. Maybe she had help from Layla and Amani?" Milo suggests.

"Maybe. I think we'll need to watch her very carefully tomorrow," I say. "This would be her last chance to get the disco cancelled."

We reach Milo's house and he opens his gate. "I'll see you tomorrow, Neesh. We'll all be on the lookout for any spooky business. We won't let anyone ruin the disco, okay?"

I plod to my house and before I even go through the door, I know we have a guest. Beena's mum's car is parked outside on the street. Not more house-moving talk!

I let myself in and I can hear Granny Jas talking very sweetly. That doesn't sound right. Last time I saw her she was marching up and down the living room with her *Granny Rights* sign! What's changed?

"Here, beta, let me show you. Look here, this one," she's saying to Mrs Bhatt.

I pop my head around the corner. "Everyone okay?" I ask cautiously.

Mum and Dad are sitting on the sofa and opposite them in the armchairs are Mrs Bhatt and Granny. I see what everyone is looking at – our old photo albums!

"Can you believe how much hair I had?" Dad exclaims.

"I know, and look how trendy I was," Mum laughs.

Granny winks at me. "Trip down memory lane," she whispers.

I've got no idea what she's up to, but it seems to be making Mum and Dad very emotional. I sit on the arm of the chair next to Granny Jas and join in flicking through the albums.

Mrs Bhatt doesn't seem as keen. "Well, as I was saying, you know these plots on the new estate won't be available for ever. The building work starts soon and most of the south-facing plots have been snapped up already," she says.

Granny opens the album on her lap. "Oh, look at this one! The day you moved into the house, beta." She holds it up to show Dad.

"We were so young and in love." He smiles at Mum. "Remember when the conservatory flooded and we had to scoop the water out with pots and pans and anything else we could find?"

Mum squeals. "You used your shoe at one point!"

Mrs Bhatt jumps in. "Well, with these new houses, you wouldn't have any problems like that."

Granny butts back in. "Oh, look, this is when you painted Anni's room before she was born."

She shows me a picture of Mum, heavily pregnant and wearing dungarees and a bright yellow scarf in her hair, happily holding a paintbrush. Her eyes are sparkling. I look at Mum now. She has that same look, like she's right back there in the picture. Dad looks like he's welling up. What is going on?

"It's only a photo!" I say.

Granny gives me a stern look. "A picture paints a thousand words," she says wisely.

I watch as Mum and Dad look back over all our memories: me learning to walk in the garden; Granny putting out the washing and me poking my head through the sheets; my first day at school. Mum and Dad washing the car and getting the bubbles everywhere; all the family birthdays and parties; Aunty Bindi and Uncle Tony's wedding. Even I feel a bit emotional! If we did move, there would be so much I'd miss about this house. Mum seems to sense what I'm thinking and says, "This house has been good to us."

Dad nods and wipes his eyes. "It really has," he agrees.

"Then we should stay – there's nothing wrong with this house!" Granny says. And right then I see what she's up to. By showing them all our happiest times in the house, she's hoping it will make them change their mind. Genius Granny!

Mrs Bhatt clears her throat loudly. "I, um... I think I'll have that tea now, if you don't mind, Auntie."*

Granny huffs but gets up to make some tea.

Mrs Bhatt quickly turns to Dad. "Mr Mistry, I know it's hard to say goodbye to a lifetime of memories, but imagine all the new memories you'll make in your brand-new, twice-as-big luxury house!" She grins like a shark.

I don't like it. I decide to change the subject before Dad can fall under her spell. "So, Mrs Bhatt.

*** Mrs Bhatt calls my granny Auntie because in our culture anyone who is older than you is automatically called aunty or uncle as a sign of respect even though they're not actually related to us. Another weird grown-up rule!**

Beena's birthday's tomorrow, isn't it? How's the party-planning coming?"

Mrs Bhatt frowns. "Well, I'd do anything for my Beena, but honestly this party has been a nightmare! I said to her, why don't you just celebrate with your friends at the school disco? But she wouldn't have it. Now she's upset because no one has replied to the invitation, not even those two airheads she calls friends, Layla and Amani! Beena made me book this expensive band – the Ghals? Gills? Ghouls? Anyway, I booked them and then last night she's crying into her pillow, saying no matter what she does the party is going to be a disaster." Mrs Bhatt throws her hands in the air. "I even tried to cheer her up by buying her a special Halloween costume to dress up in this week. It's a lovely orange pumpkin, very festive I thought and it's sparkly! I thought she could either wear it to her party or just come to the disco but she bit my head off! I notice she took the costume and the wig anyway, though, so maybe there's some hope."

"Wig?" I ask, my mind whirring now. "It wouldn't be orange, would it? To match the outfit?"

"Yes, actually. I regret buying it though, that wig leaves hairs everywhere! All over my car on my nice upholstery!"

My heart is thudding in my chest. Just then Granny Jas comes back with the tea and Mum starts talking to Mrs Bhatt about how fast we kids have grown up and how the birthdays roll around so quickly.

Mrs Bhatt sighs. "They do, but you know birthdays are never a happy time for Beena. It doesn't seem to matter how many presents she gets or how big the cake is. She wants the biggest, boldest parties, but then none of her school friends come anyway and it's just all us oldies and cousin Pritpal on the dance floor doing dance moves from the eighties. I feel bad for her, but she shrugs it off. I never understand why no one comes and she won't talk to me. Do you know, Anisha?"

My face feels hot. How do I even answer that? I can't admit it's because Beena is a horrible person. So instead I say, "Well, I think maybe the school disco being on the same day this year hasn't helped. I'm sure lots of people would have wanted to come if it wasn't for that."

Mrs Bhatt nods. "Yes, Beena was most upset about the disco, actually." She looks off into the distance for a moment. "You know, Anisha, I wish Beena had more friends like you." She smiles sadly.

I think everyone feels awkward now, so I try and change the subject again. "Hey, Dad – tell Mrs Bhatt about the disaster we had at my sixth birthday party with that weird clown entertainer person!"

As Dad starts his story, I excuse myself and leave the living room. The feeling that Beena is behind the fake ghost stuff has been creeping up on me all afternoon.

Look, her mum said it – she never has any friends from school at her parties. Maybe she thought if she ruined the disco, we'd just come to her party instead? But then how did she manage all the trickery by herself?

I need to check one thing before I do anything else. Mrs Bhatt said there are orange hairs from Beena's wig all over her car. If I can get hold of one of those hairs and match it to the ones we found in the library and in Fang's cage, I can prove Beena is behind all this. But how do I get into Mrs Bhatt's car without being seen?

I go upstairs to my room and sit on my bed, wondering what to do now. I get out my notebook and write:

Evidence against Beena Bhatt:

- **Orange hairs could tie Beena to the catapult in the library and the person we saw running away from the pumpkin pyramid.**
- **Beena was sitting closest to Skeleton Fred when he moved in the science lab.**
- **She wasn't afraid of Fang and told Maryam not to be scared of him, so she could have been the one who let Fang out! (There was an orange hair in his tank too.)**
- **When she heard the school might be closed down she seemed to freak out**

more than anyone else. Could that be a sign of guilt?

- **She has been so eager for everyone to come to her party and her mum said how upset she's been about no one going. That's a pretty good motive.**

The more I write, the more convinced I am that it's her.

Just then, Mum calls up from the hallway. "Grab your jacket, Anni, we're going to see something really exciting!"

Dad comes out too, grinning. "We're going to one of the new houses."

"Wait, what?" I exclaim. "Now?"

Mrs Bhatt comes up behind Mum and Dad. "I thought it might be nice for you all to see what you'll be moving into. It's a show home, so not the exact one, but it'll give you a good idea. It's really nice." She smiles.

Granny huffs and folds her arms. "I'm **NOT** going!"

I want to say no too but then Mrs Bhatt says, "We can go in my car!"

And then I know I *have* to go, because this is my chance to get the final proof I need against Beena!

A little while later we're driving back home. Mum and Dad don't say much on the way, but I guess they're busy thinking about the move. The show home was nice – I mean, it was okay – but it didn't feel like our home and it felt really far away even though it's in our city. It is bigger and fancier than our house. I felt like Mum and Dad were impressed;

they gawped a lot and nodded a lot as Mrs Bhatt showed us around. But even though I'm still so worried about moving, I have to put it to one side for now and solve this mystery. If Mum and Dad are set on moving, then this might be the last thing I do for my friends and my school – saving the disco – saving the school!

What with Dad's constant chattering on the way to the house though, I didn't even get to look around in Mrs Bhatt's car. Finally now I look around in the back of Mrs Bhatt's car. Nothing on the seats, nothing in the side of the car door. Then I look in front of me at the passenger seat where Mum is sitting. Against her dark hair I can see a streak of orange! It's a single hair, stuck in the headrest! I reach forward and grab it, quickly stuffing it in my pocket. Dad looks over at me but doesn't say anything. He seems distracted.

As soon as we get inside our house, the grown-ups go into the living room and I run up to my room.

I need to compare the hair from the car and the hair we found in school.

I put the two hairs together on a piece of white paper. They are identical! This proves it's Beena! I need to talk to Milo about all this.

I'm about to go downstairs when I hear Mrs Bhatt answering her phone. She's talking to Beena.

"Hi, Beena, sweetheart, how was your day? … Yes, I'm coming home now… Of course you can go into school early tomorrow – but why? … Really? … You've decided to help with the Halloween decorations? … That's nice, darling. I'm glad you're feeling much better about it all... And we'll have a lovely family birthday party for you, okay? Cousin Pritpal is bringing his karaoke machine too... Okay, beta, I'll see you in a bit."

She hangs up and then carries on talking to Mum and Dad. "I'll need you to let me know tomorrow. I can only keep the house for you until then," she says.

"Okay, we have some things to think about. Thank you for coming," I hear Dad say.

I flinch at the news that Mum and Dad only have until tomorrow to confirm that they want the other house. Can't get distracted now though. I let them finish and then I grab my backpack and run downstairs.

"Um...Anni, sweetheart, can we talk to you?" Mum asks.

"Can we do it later, Mum? I really need to get to Milo's. We've got stuff to get ready for tomorrow." It's not a total lie.

"Really? Okay, but we do need to talk," says Dad,

turning to go into the kitchen with Mum.

Granny gives me a quick hug. "Everything okay, beta? Can't have been easy to go and see the new house. I hope your parents come to their senses soon."

"Yeah, it will be okay, Granny," I say. "By the way, very sneaky with the photos! I'm not sure how much good it's done though." I sigh.

"I'm not done yet – Granny has ways!" She winks and laughs.

I run down to Milo's and knock on the door. He answers dressed in his PJs and fluffy slippers which have lion faces on them.

"Oh, Neesh! I wasn't expecting you. Everything okay?" he asks.

"Yeah, well, no, but kind of. I know who's behind all the haunting at school, Milo. It **WAS** Beena! And I have proof! Plus I know how we can catch her. She's told her mum she wants to go into school early tomorrow to help with the decorations. You know what that means?"

"She's going to be helpful for once?" Milo asks.

"No, it's clearly a lie! She's planning a last big attempt to ruin things and get the disco cancelled once and for all," I say. "And we're going to stop her!"

CHAPTER THIRTEEN

THE TRAP

The next morning, I get up and get ready for school early. Dad's still in the shower and Mum is buzzing about the living room like an excited wasp.

"Are you okay, Mum?" I ask as I grab my bag.

Granny gives Mum a strange look. "Oh, she's just excited for the salsa performance later. We'll see you at the disco, beta. Have a good day – you'd better be going now." And she practically pushes me out of the house, shoving a piece of toast at me for my breakfast. What is going on?

I hear Mum protesting, "I wasn't going to say anything!"

Granny says, "I hope not, you have to wait for everyone else to be here."

Probably more bad house news then, I think, and my tummy turns at the thought of it. No time to worry about it now though – I'll have to deal with one problem at a time!

Milo and I get to school early and find Mindy and Manny. I called them last night to tell them to meet us. I fill them in on what's happening.

"I can't believe it's Beena. Well, I can, but still... so sneaky!" Manny says.

"But it stops today!" I say. "Okay, so Beena seems to strike every time we're doing some sort of preparation for the disco, right?"

Milo nods. "Right."

"And today is the day of the disco, so I bet she'll have one last go at sabotaging it while we're putting up the decorations we've made and getting the hall ready. Even though she seemed worried about what Mrs Afzal said yesterday, I think she's still desperate to get us all to go to her party instead."

"It's all a bit daft really, isn't it? She could have just told us how she was feeling," Mindy says.

"Well, yeah, but I don't think that's Beena's style," I say.

"Maybe it will be after this?" Manny suggests hopefully.

"Hmm, I wouldn't count on it," I reply.

"Well, we're right with you, Anisha." Mindy smiles. She looks really happy today, like, more than usual.

"Has something happened?" I ask. "You're very smiley."

Mindy goes a bit red in the face and glances at Manny, who is also grinning. "No, well, yeah, but we're not allowed to say. It'll make sense later. Anyway, let's get this disco sorted first!"

My whole family is being very secretive this morning. I make a mental note to investigate that further once we've sorted out Beena.

Mindy, Milo, Manny and I go to find Mr Graft to ask if we can start decorating the hall.

He's dressing up Skeleton Fred in a pirate's hat and costume and Ghastly Gertrude is wearing a floaty dress which looks like someone's old curtains. He just waves us away. "Yes, yes, carry on. I have to get these two ready, there's so much to do!"

"I'm kind of scared about what Beena's going to do to us," Milo murmurs as we walk.

"It won't be anything that scary – we know she's not a real ghost," Mindy says.

"No, I know that. I meant, what is she going to do to us when she realizes that we've caught her?" Milo says.

All the decorations are being kept in the hall, so we head straight there. It's 8 a.m., so the school is still pretty quiet since the bell doesn't ring till 9 a.m.

I look around and check behind the door. "All clear! She hasn't come in yet," I say. "We have to work quickly if we're going to catch her in the act though – she could arrive any minute."

We lay the decorations out in the centre of the hall as if someone is getting ready to put them up. Beena won't be able to resist sabotaging them.

"Manny, have you got the camera on your phone ready to record?" I ask. But before he has a chance to reply, we hear footsteps coming down the hall. Quickly, we all find a place to hide behind the curtains on the stage. The door to the hall opens and we freeze, listening.

I try to see through the crack in the curtains. I catch a flash of the orange wig and Beena's face under it! This confirms it for definite!

Milo is scratching his nose next to me and Manny is fidgeting. Beena is going to realize we're here if they don't stop. I nudge Milo and glare at him. He nudges Manny, who almost falls forward through the curtain.

I shake my head and look back through the gap. Beena has totally ignored our decorations trap and is hauling herself up the climbing frame, which is attached to the wall nearest to the door. **WHAT** is she doing? She positions herself in a most precarious way – she is balancing on the climbing frame and

holding a stick. That's when I notice there's a bucket balanced up there on the top window ledge. She's trying to hook the bucket onto her stick – what is she doing that for? Her orange wig is flopping over her eyes and she's now hanging with one arm stretched out and one leg wobbling about. We come out from behind the curtain and watch her.

"**BEENA!** What are you doing!" Mindy shouts, which startles Beena. Her head snaps round to look at us but at the same time her grip on the climbing frame slips and her legs flail about as she struggles to keep hold of the bar with one arm. Her other hand is still holding onto the stick, which now has the bucket dangling from it.

"You have to let go of the stick, Beena!" I shout. "You're going to fall if you don't let go of it!"

"I can't! The bucket!" Beena strains. She stretches her arm and moves it slowly but the bucket is dangling above her head. As the bucket starts to tip, I can see what's going to happen, but I can't stop it!

SPLOSH!

Green slimes pours out, all over Beena's head! Her scream is so high-pitched it makes us all cover our ears:

CHAPTER FOURTEEN

CONFESSIONS OF A FAKE GHOST

Once the shock of Beena sliming herself wears off, we leap into action and run to help her. We pull a padded PE mat out and place it underneath her just in case. Beena is not ready to accept help though and yells at us.

"Stay back!" she screams.

"We're just trying to help!" I shout back. "We don't have to, you know! *You* are the one who was trying to slime the disco and ended up sliming yourself."

Beena grips the climbing frame harder for safety. She looks down at us, shocked, then angry and then

scared. "It's not what it looks like! I was trying to take the slime down," she shouts.

"Beena, come on, just tell the truth! We know it's you who's been pretending to be a ghost. You just got caught slime-handed!" I say.

Beena huffs. "I really was taking it down. Can I at least explain, or have you already made your minds up as usual?"

"You can try to explain but I still have to tell Mr Graft what you've been up to. You tried to make everyone think the school was haunted. All because you wanted to spoil the disco!"

"You're such a goody two shoes, Anisha!" Beena stares at me, slime dripping down her face. "I need to get down first. It's not easy hanging off here by one arm!"

"Should be easier now you've emptied that bucket," Mindy remarks, glaring at Beena.

"Urgh, hilarious, Mindy. Like you never did anything wrong in your life," Beena says pointedly as she clambers down, globs of gloop falling from her onto the floor.

Mindy just stares right back. "Yeah, actually I have made some mistakes, but I realized I was wrong and I made up for them. You just go round thinking you're the queen of everything!"

Beena blinks. "Well, you used to be friends with me, not these losers. What's that all about?"

"Look, none of this is helping," I say. "Beena, what's going on? You must know this isn't the way to make friends, right?"

"Who said I want any stupid friends at this school anyway – you're **ALL** losers!" Beena shouts, ripping off her slimy orange wig. Then she plonks herself on the floor and bursts into tears!

Mindy, Manny and I all stand around awkwardly, not really knowing what to do. I've never seen Beena cry or show any emotion except for anger. But Milo knows what to do – he always does. He crouches down and puts his arm around her. Beena looks up, glares at him, but doesn't push him away.

"It wasn't meant to go this far," she sniffles. "But no one ever gives my parties a chance. I bugged my mum to book the band, thinking that would make more people want to come – but then the school announced the disco and I knew I had no chance. I knew about the ghost legend and when Maryam started telling people too, I realized people lap that sort of stuff up, don't they? I thought I could use it as a way to scare people away from the disco. Look, I know it probably wasn't the best idea in the history of ideas...and I also know I'm not the easiest person to be friends with."

Mindy snorts.

"Yeah, okay, I can be horrible, I know that. I don't mean to be...well, not always, but that's not the point. I was going to be nice. I had it all planned out – I was including everyone in my party, even you losers. I mean, you lot. But with everyone all hyped about the disco, I knew I needed to do something."

"So you started messing with Skeleton Fred first. How did you do that? I'm curious!" I say. "I checked all round him and there was no clue that someone had been controlling him."

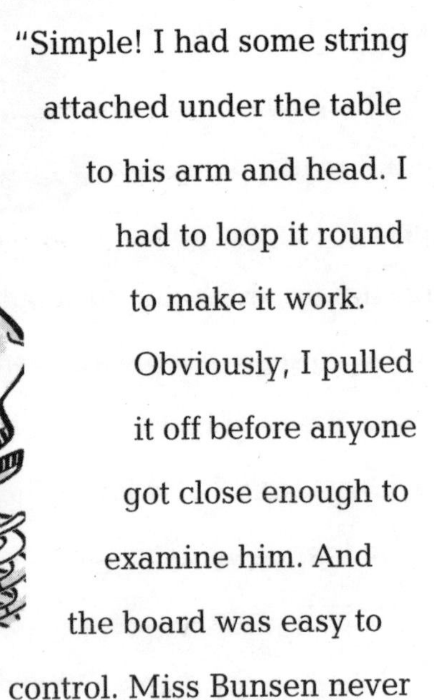

"Simple! I had some string attached under the table to his arm and head. I had to loop it round to make it work. Obviously, I pulled it off before anyone got close enough to examine him. And the board was easy to control. Miss Bunsen never puts the remote back properly – she didn't even notice it was missing. I was controlling that under the desk too. I'd been into class a bit earlier to set it up. The lights were just playing up, I don't know why but it was just good timing for me!"

"Evil genius," Milo murmurs.

"Why, thank you." Beena smiles.

"It's not anything to be proud of," I say.

"Well, it fooled most of the class, didn't it?" Beena retorts.

"I knew it wasn't a real ghost after you made the books fly across the library – which, by the way, was destructive and dangerous!" I say. "You slipped up when you left the catapult at the scene of the crime. Not very supernatural."

"Yeah, I was annoyed that I dropped it when Mr Graft evacuated everyone," Beena admits. "I didn't realize till later and it was too late to go back.

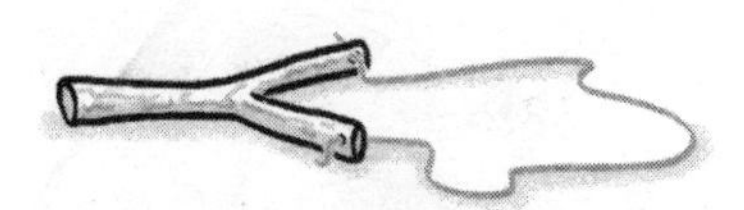

"How did you get the slime into the canteen?" Mindy asks. "That caused chaos!"

"I was kind of proud of that part of the plan," Beena says. "I made it myself! Then on that day I came in early. The dinner staff don't start till after first bell, so the kitchen was empty. I smuggled the bucket of slime in and poured it into one of the big pans. Then at lunchtime I popped back and positioned it so the dinner staff would use it. I let Fang out from his tank and put him in the canteen."

"But it caused so much mess and Mr Graft was furious," I say. "Plus, it still didn't make anyone want to go to your party, Beena! So what was the point!"

"Well, I didn't know that people would start throwing food – I'm not responsible for the silly things they all did. I was desperate, Anisha. You don't know what it's like to feel like this, because most people actually like you," Beena says, her voice full of resentment.

"Maybe they would like you more if you weren't so mean all the time." Milo shrugs.

Beena looks down.

I touch her arm. "Look, what's done is done. The truth is out now. I take it the pumpkin prank was a last attempt to scare everyone off the school disco?"

Beena nods. "It didn't really work though, because you found it first and then I thought you'd seen me by the window. It's all been a total disaster really."

"I didn't know it was you, I just saw the orange wig from what I'm guessing is the pumpkin costume your mum bought for you," I say. "It was actually your mum that put me onto you, because she mentioned the costume when she was at our house."

Beena rolls her eyes. "Great, thanks, Mum! So, what now? You tell Mr Graft and I get in trouble. I guess the upside is that my mum will probably cancel the party when she hears what I've done, so I won't need to worry about no one turning up."

"Maybe if you say you're sorry and try to make things right, it might help?" Mindy suggests.

Beena considers this for a moment. "Do you think so? I know I don't always go about stuff in the right way. I suppose I just get lonely sometimes. I guess I got a bit carried away with the ghost stuff. I just wanted to have a good birthday for once."

"I didn't realize you felt lonely, Beena – but that's not an excuse. And don't you actually have friends – Layla and Amani?" Milo asks.

"Yeah, I have Layla and Amani, but I sometimes think they just put up with me and actually get on better with each other anyway."

"Wow, I would never have guessed you felt like that, and they probably don't realize either, Beena. You should talk to them. I don't think they would follow you around like they do if they didn't care at all," says Milo.

"Anyway, what were you up to just now? Was this a last attempt to ruin things by sliming the hall?" asks Mindy.

"That's just it! I was trying to take the slime down! I put it up there yesterday and then had second thoughts when I spoke to Maryam's mum. I realized I went way over the top – I never wanted to risk getting the whole school shut down! I just wanted this one disco to get cancelled. I was trying to do the right thing for once."

"Wow, if that's true then that's kind of amazing, you know. It takes guts to admit you're wrong and then also try to fix things – even if you could have done it a bit sooner!" I say.

"Well, it's really not amazing because no one will want to be my friend now, will they? Everyone was so excited about the school disco and I tried to ruin it. Plus, look – there's slime everywhere. Mr Graft is going to be so angry!" Beena says, looking even more worried.

"Okay, one thing at a time," I say. "If you're genuinely sorry, I think we can help you make this right."

"Why would you help me?" Beena sniffs.

"Yeah, why **WOULD** we help her?" Mindy asks.

"Everyone deserves a second chance, Mindy," I say. "Plus, it would be nice if something good came out of all this." I gesture to the slime-covered Beena.

Mindy smiles slightly. "Okay, okay, we'll help. But, Beena, I'm serious – you'd better not be mean to any of us ever again!"

Beena nods quickly. "I promise. I think I'm done being mean."

Milo looks at me, wide-eyed, and mouths the word, "**WOW!**"

I mouth back, "I know!"

"Right, what's first then?" Mindy asks.

"Well, the disco is in just over six hours and there's slime everywhere. We'd better get some help if we're going to make this party happen!" I say.

CHAPTER FIFTEEN

MAKING IT RIGHT

We have to move quickly after Beena's confession. She surprises us all by calling her mum and telling her everything. She gets a right telling-off, but I think in a way she's relieved to tell the truth.

"I'm going to put it right, Mum, I promise," we hear her say.

Then she goes off in a corner to carry on talking to her mum. She's gesturing a lot and I hope her mum will forgive her. She does seem to be very sorry for what she did.

"What shall we do now?" Mindy asks. "The hall is a right mess!"

"We're going to need help," I say. "Let's get Mr Graft and Mr Bristles and anyone else we can find."

Beena comes back then. "I would never have thought it, but I feel so much better for telling on myself, weirdly," she admits.

"I'm glad," I say. "We were just saying we need to get Mr Graft and Mr Bristles to help clean all this up. But that means telling the truth to the teachers too, Beena. Are you up for that?" I ask.

Beena smiles. "You know what, I think I am."

So, we find Mr Graft and Beena tells her story. He frowns a lot as she speaks and shakes his head and at the end, I think he might explode but he doesn't. A couple of times, he asks her to slow down and go back and explain something. He stays quite calm throughout actually.

"Beena, you realize how much trouble you've caused, don't you? You almost ruined the disco for everyone at school. Not to mention the slime incident, which could have had more serious consequences!"

Beena nods and looks at the floor. "I know, sir, I was wrong. I don't have any excuses. I just want to help fix things now. The rest of the school shouldn't be punished for what I did."

"That's very mature of you, Beena. I appreciate it. Right, well you can start by tidying yourself up and then fetching some cleaning equipment from Mr Bristles and getting to work on that slime all over the hall floor," he replies sternly.

"We will all need to pitch in and get things ready for later. I take it our ghost has finally left the building?" he asks with his eyebrows raised.

"Yes, sir, no more haunting, I promise." Beena smiles sheepishly.

Mr Graft excuses us from all our morning lessons so we can help clear up and get everything ready. Mr Graft gets Skeleton Fred and Ghastly Gertrude and positions them up at the front of the hall with the big banner. Beena then pulls out a bag of surprises – she's brought in *more* decorations to make up for the chaos she caused in the week. There are some really nice ones in there: a chain of rainbow-coloured skeletons, a glittery Halloween banner and some really cool lights – plus there's

a whole bag of dress-up accessories. Beena even starts to get into it a bit, trying out the different masks and some monster hands.

"See, you don't hate Halloween," I say to her.

"No, I guess not," Beena says, smiling the biggest and most genuine smile I've ever seen on her face.

What with sorting out the hall and then a couple of our normal afternoon lessons, the day goes by really quickly. Everyone gets to finish at 2.30 p.m. so they can change for the disco which is at 3 p.m.

"I kind of wish I was staying now." Beena sighs. "You are all going to have so much fun."

"Stay then! I'm sure your mum wouldn't mind asking your relatives to come to your house a bit later," I say.

"Yeah, probably, but I don't even have anything to wear with me. It's fancy dress, remember, and my costume is at home. I stuffed it into my bin last night when I was upset about everything," Beena tells me.

Just then her mum pops her head round the door. "I think I can help with that!" she says, holding up an outfit on a hanger.

It's a big sparkly foam pumpkin costume!

"After we spoke I thought

you might want to stay for the disco after all so I brought it just in case," Mrs Bhatt explains.

"Haha, oh my gosh, you got it out of my bin! It doesn't even look crumpled!" Beena hoots. "Mum, thank you! Are you sure I can stay? Won't everyone at home be disappointed?"

"Well, no, I explained you're celebrating with your friends this year and we'll see them at the weekend instead. Cousin Pritpal was a bit upset, but I promised he could do a karaoke solo when we do see him."

"So, I guess I'm staying!" Beena squeals excitedly but then she stops. "Oh, is that okay with all of you? I mean, I would understand if you didn't want me to be here. I did almost ruin the disco for everyone."

We all look at each other and try to keep straight faces. Beena looks worried, but then we crack up. "Yes, Beena, we'd like you to stay!" we shout.

Suddenly, my heart sinks. I realize then that I don't have a costume. What with everything else going on, I totally forgot!

"Milo, I didn't sort out my—" I start to say.

Milo grins, holding something behind his back. "Are you looking for this?" he asks. He pulls out a costume – it's a boiler suit with my name on the pocket!

"Spookbusters!" I shout. "Did your nan really make this?"

"Yeah, she's awesome. Look at the badge she sewed on." Milo points proudly. It's a green and orange badge that says *Ghosts Beware!*

"I love it," I say.

Mindy and Manny have identical outfits too, and we all head off to get changed. We're so excited. Before things get started, I find Mrs Bhatt. "Can I ask you something? I have an idea," I say.

A few minutes later I rejoin my friends. The hall looks **SPOOKTACULAR!** All the decorated

pumpkins are lined up around the edge of the room and there are little orange and green lights hanging everywhere. The decorations we made in class look so spooky too – there're just the right amount of creepy cobwebs! There's a long table

with food and drinks on it, including giant bowls of popcorn and funny little jelly sweets shaped like ghosts.

The teachers have gone all out for the disco too. I've never seen them looking so funny! Mr Graft's costume is brilliant. He's Frankenstein – or, as he keeps correcting everyone, Frankenstein's Monster. He has a big hat on his head to make it look square, his face is green and he's stuck two bolts either side of his neck! Miss Bunsen's bright green hair doesn't look so strange now everyone else is dressed up too. It kind of blends in and she looks really cool! Even Mr Bristles has dressed up – he's wearing his Dracula costume from his part-time job at the theme park. I'd forgotten he had that!

Mr Fields, our PE teacher, is in charge of music

and he's taking it very seriously. He's wearing giant headphones and holding a microphone that he keeps shouting into. "DJ Fields, on the mic. One two, one two!"

As the hall fills up, we stand back and admire everyone's costumes – there are quite a few super heroes, some skeletons and one unfortunate wardrobe disaster for a kid who has come as a scary storybook: his pages are so wide and keep flapping about and he has to move around sideways to get

through the crowd. I kind of like his style though.

Mr Graft comes over to speak to us. "Well, Anisha, you did it again! You saved the day!"

My face feels a bit hot. "It's not a big deal, sir."

"It most certainly is," Mr Graft says. "If not for you and your intrepid investigations, our disco could have been cancelled and all future parties too, maybe even our school shut down for good! The school owes you a big debt of gratitude," he declares solemnly.

"Does that mean we can have Monday off school, sir?" Manny asks cheekily.

"Erm, let me think...that would be a **NO**!" Mr Graft answers firmly and marches away to tell one of the other kids to stop jumping on his friend.

"Worth a try." Manny shrugs and goes off to the food table with Milo to get some popcorn.

"Happy you stuck around for the disco?" Mindy asks me. "These costumes aren't so bad and hopefully Beena has learned her lesson finally!"

"I am glad to be here actually," I say. "And do you know, it's weird, but I think I understand Beena a lot better now. She's not so bad."

"Are you serious, Anisha?" Mindy splutters.

"Yeah, I really do think we're going to see a different Beena from now on," I say.

"Okay, well I'm not convinced but let's hope so," Mindy says.

Just then I see Beena onstage, gesturing to Mr Fields to stop the music.

"Oh, here we go, you were saying about her being different?" Mindy points.

Beena takes the microphone and, for a second, I think she might not have changed at all. She always has to be centre of attention! But she stares at us for a moment and then breaks into a smile.

"Hi, everyone. I...um...look, I haven't been my best self recently, and I did some silly things that got out of hand. Anyway, I've apologized, but I know I need to do more than that, so this is a small gesture from me to everyone here. I want you to meet some very special guests. They were supposed to perform at my birthday party, but I realized it would be so much more fun if I got to share them with all of you! So, I called my mum and asked her to make a slight change to our booking and without any more messing about, here are... **THE GHOULS!**"

Beena walks offstage and the lights go down. Four singers step out, dressed in costume. The music starts up and they sing "Monster Mash", pointing to everyone in the audience.

"I can't believe she got The Ghouls here!" Mindy says, impressed.

"I know, that's the nicest thing I've ever seen her do," I reply.

"This disco is the best thing ever to happen in our school." Mindy laughs.

"You might be right," I say. "It's not over yet though!"

CHAPTER SIXTEEN

SALSA SPECTACULAR!

I realize I kind of love The Ghouls' music. They do a mix of old songs and their own stuff, and soon I'm tapping my foot along to the beat. Then Mindy drags me to the dance floor, where we do our own little shuffle before Milo and Manny come jumping in. Someone starts doing a side-to-side step and making zombie hands and soon we're all doing it.

It's actually quite fun. I'm not the most co-ordinated person, but it kind of doesn't matter when you're pretending to be a zombie!

After The Ghouls have done their set, Mr Fields takes over again. I see Beena's mum is signalling me to say it's time for the surprise I spoke to her about earlier. I jump up onstage and tell Mr Fields what we've got planned and he agrees to help.

"Just need to find that one special song," he says, rummaging in his crate of big round discs.

"I thought you had your music on computer," I say.

"Oh no! You can't beat playing a proper good old-fashioned record. The sound is completely different. I've had these since I was a boy – they were my dad's!" he replies. "Ah, here it is. Right, you make the announcement and I'll get this lined up to play."

I take the microphone and step out onto centre stage nervously. Speaking to an audience of monsters and spooky creatures is not something I thought I'd ever do. The light shines in my eyes,

so I can't see everyone's faces properly. That might be a good thing – I hate speaking in public. This is for a good reason though. I can do this. I clear my throat and Mr Fields cuts the music. Everyone turns and looks at me.

"Um...hi, everyone. I just wanted to ask you all to share something special with me. Today is the first disco our school has had in years and that's really cool and I hope everyone is having a great time. But it's also a special day for someone else here and I think we can celebrate both things. Beena, would you come up here, please?"

Beena looks horrified and shakes her head at me, but her friends Layla and Amani nudge her forward.

Beena walks to the stage reluctantly and when she's standing next to me she whispers, "There's really no need for this."

I ignore her and continue. "It's Beena's birthday today and you have to have cake on your birthday, right?"

Everyone cheers and then I give Mr Fields the thumbs up to play the music. The "Happy Birthday" song starts up and we all sing along. From the far end of the hall, Beena's mum comes in, pushing a trolley which is carrying the biggest cake I've ever seen. It's a three-tier raspberry and chocolate sponge and it has frosting and sprinkles all round the edges. On the top is a big cake sparkler and Beena's name

in gold icing. Beena is grinning from ear to ear.

"I can't believe you brought my cake here!" she yells. She jumps down off the stage and hugs her mum.

We finish singing and someone shouts, "Make a wish!"

Beena closes her eyes, whispers a wish, and then gives it everything she's got to blow out the candles. We all cheer again and Beena's mum gives her another big hug. I see Mr Graft blinking back a tear and then he looks over at me. He gives me a nod, as if to say, *Good job*.

Then Beena runs over to me and gives me a hug too! I'm a bit shocked, but she looks genuinely over the moon and I feel happy for her.

"That's the nicest thing anyone has ever done for me," she says. "Thank you, Anisha, for not seeing the worst in me and for believing I can be better."

I just nod, because there's a weird lump in my throat and I can't get any words out suddenly.

There's an awkward silence and then Beena says, "It's been a pretty good party, Anisha. I think maybe I was wrong about you all this time."

"Wow, are you sure, Beena?" I laugh.

Beena laughs too. "I know, I know. Look, you made my birthday pretty much the best one I've had, so thank you. Maybe we can be friends from now on?"

"I'll still be keeping a close eye on you," Mindy

warns as she comes to stand by my side.

"I know," Beena replies. "Being nice all the time won't be easy, but I want to try."

"Well, that's a start. And yes, if you mean it I'd like it if we can be friends," I agree. In my head I'm thinking it's a shame it's taken this long for us to be friends, because now that we are, I might be moving house anyway. I don't say it though – I don't want to ruin the moment.

After everyone has wished Beena "Happy Birthday" and she's stopped hugging us all, it's finally time for the special performance by the grown-ups. Only Mindy, Manny, Milo and I know about this, so when the music is turned down and a spotlight focuses on the stage, everyone goes quiet – while we prepare to cringe hard!

Suddenly there is an explosion of confetti and a beat starts up. Out steps Mr Graft, wiggling his hips. Everyone gasps and cheers, realizing this is not your average school dance. Mr Graft is beaming and gestures to the line of dancers behind him. I can see my parents, both dressed as ghosts, Aunty Bindi, who is the most sparkly skeleton I have ever seen, and Uncle Tony dressed as Dracula, who smiles sheepishly, showing his fangs. Granny Jas is dressed very differently to how I normally see her. She's a werewolf! She winks at me as she poses with one hand on her hip.

"Oh wow, are you seeing this?" Mindy murmurs.

"Unfortunately, yes," I reply. "I think this might be the scariest Halloween surprise of all!"

"Is that your mum, Anisha?" someone shouts.

"Ground, swallow me up!" I whisper to myself.

They all start to move to the music and some of them dance in pairs. It's not so cringey once it gets going. I notice some of the kids start to sway along too. This song is quite catchy! And don't tell them I said this but...my parents actually look good! Dad has got some moves! Mum steps back and forth in time with him, and they really look like they're having fun. I think back to their happy photos in the album – they look like that again now.

Aunty Bindi is, of course, centre stage and she seems to be leading Uncle Tony – he just goes where she drags him. He pulls that face that he always pulls when he's dancing, which looks like he needs the loo! But he gives me a thumbs up as they go past, so I guess he's having fun too. Mr Graft dances with Miss Bunsen and suddenly he lifts her into the air, throws her up and catches her! Woah, who knew salsa was so acrobatic?! Aunty Bindi sees this and starts nudging Uncle Tony to do the same. He shakes his head vigorously. Not doing that! No way!

I laugh to myself; I was cringing the other day when I found out my family were going to do this,

but actually they are so brave, doing something new in front of all these people. Milo's mum is there and some of the other parents too but of course my family are front and centre stage. Granny does a little solo salsa wiggle and twirl at the front of the group and everyone cheers. I never knew she could move her hips like that!

Someone whistles and shouts, "Anisha, your family rock!"

"Er...**OUR** family! Get it right! Thank you!" Mindy yells back.

I blush but I'm secretly pleased. Our family really do rock.

The dance number finishes and The Ghouls come out again and play a song everyone seems to know. It's a cover of a song called Thriller – even Mum and Dad seem to know it! Mindy, Manny and Milo come bopping over and for once I don't feel self-conscious about having a little dance. It's a Halloween miracle!

My family decide to stay for a bit, which I thought I would hate but it's actually quite fun.

All the teachers join in on the dance floor too. Miss Bunsen has some really wild moves though and almost takes out Mr Graft's eye with her pointing fingers – very bizarre and a bit scary!

Just as we're really getting into the next song, Mum and Dad come and take me to one side.

"We need to talk to you, Anni," Mum says with a serious face.

"Yeah, it's very important, it's about the house," Dad says, looking even more serious than Mum.

"Oh, that. I'd forgotten about that for a bit."

I sigh. "Does it have to be now? Oh, I suppose we should just get it over with. Go on then, what is it? You've sold the house already?" I ask.

Mum and Dad look at each other and then me. They break into smiles.

"No, Anni, that's just it, we're not moving! We're staying in our lovely house and keeping things as they are," Mum says.

"We're not moving? But I thought that's what you wanted? You put the house up for sale and everything!" I exclaim.

"Yes, we thought it was what we wanted, but we could see you didn't, and it was making everyone so unhappy. And, you know, your Granny Jas has a way of making us

come round to her way of thinking."

"The photo albums?" I smile.

"Yes, the photo albums." Mum grins. "And when we went to see the other house, we realized it just didn't have the character our house has. It was all very fancy and nice but it wouldn't be the same. We've let Mrs Bhatt know – she kind of had a feeling anyway. Plus, we also had some other news which made us think it would be a good idea to stick around and stay close to our family. There are some exciting things happening right here."

"What?" I ask.

Just then Aunty Bindi comes over with Mindy and Manny.

Manny beams. "Have you told her yet?" he asks excitedly.

"Told me what?" I ask. "Why is this family always keeping secrets?"

Aunty Bindi laughs. "Well. We wanted to be sure first."

"Sure about what?" I ask. "How come Manny knows what it is?"

"I know too." Mindy grins.

Uncle Tony looks like he's going to burst. "We're having a baby!" he yells.

Aunty Bindi squeals. "You're going to have another cousin!"

My heart leaps. A baby! That's so exciting! But then I look at Mindy and Manny. I need to make sure they're okay. "A baby! Wow. How do you both feel about this?"

Mindy smiles. "We love it, Anisha. You showed us how great it is to have a big family. And I've always wanted to be a big sister!"

I hug Mindy and Manny piles onto us too.

Milo comes leaping over. "If we're hugging, I want to join in too!" he says.

I look up at Mum and Dad – they both have tears in their eyes. I don't normally like mushy moments, but this is a good one.

Granny Jas joins us and nudges me. "You see, everything works out in the end. And I will have another grandchild – this one I think will like my brown daal. Not like the rest of you lot! So picky!"

Mindy, Manny and I look at each other. "Eww, brown daal!" we all shout and start laughing.

"So rude, these kids!" Granny huffs but she's laughing too.

The rest of the disco is a blur as we chat excitedly about the baby and what the new addition to our family might be like. I'm going to be a big cousin, almost like a big sister too. I feel really happy. Our family is getting bigger, we don't have to move house and Beena Bhatt is not going to be mean any more. Life is pretty good right now. I can't believe how much has changed since this morning!

As the disco is winding down and people start leaving, or are just chatting or picking at the last bits of food, I sit on a chair and take a minute. Mr Graft spots me and comes over.

"Do my eyes deceive me or did you actually have a very good time at that party, Anisha Mistry?" He smiles.

"I think I did," I agree. "Strange, isn't it?"

"Well, this is a brilliant development! If that's the case, on Monday we'll start planning the Christmas party, okay?" He beams.

I feel all the blood drain from my face. "Really? I don't know about that, Mr Graft. I'm probably not the right person and I really don't think we should rush into anything. I mean we just about pulled this party off. Maybe we should give it a rest till like, next year, or the year after?" I scramble, trying to think of excuses.

"No, I think you make a great party-planner, Anisha, you have a lot of skill. And you are great at keeping things on track. Plus…" He shrugs and does a little salsa wiggle. "What could possibly go wrong at Christmas?!"

MAKE YOUR OWN SLIME!

Okay, I'll admit it – the slime fight in the canteen was fun! But did you know that slime is also great for this fun and easy home science experiment.

YOU WILL NEED:

- A cup of cornflour
- A half a cup of water
- A few drops of food dye* (green for the spookiest slime!)
- A mixing bowl

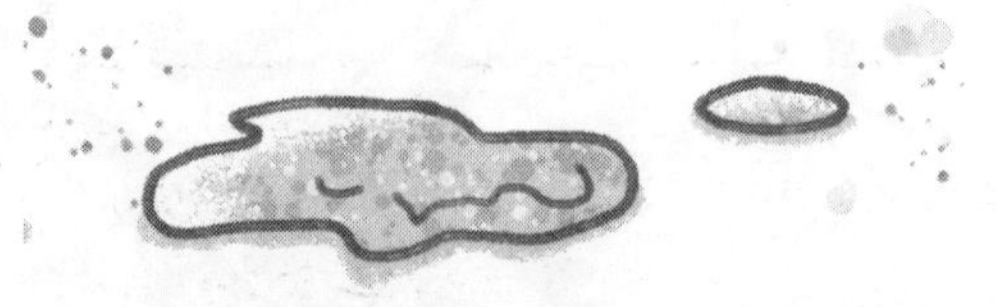

*** You might want to wear an apron if you're using this – things might get messy!**

Why don't you ask a grown-up to help you?

1. Add the food dye to the water and mix until the water is coloured.
2. Pour the cornflour into the bowl.
3. Slowly add the water to the cornflour.
4. Using your fingers, mix the water into the cornflour until you can't see any dry lumps.

TOP TIP!
If the slime feels too runny, add more cornflour

Okay – now for the **SCIENCE BIT!**

- **Tip** the bowl slowly from side to side. How does the mixture **move**?
- **Hit** the top of the slime with the back of a spoon. Does the spoon **squish** into the slime or **bounce off**?

WHY DOES THE SLIME DO THIS?

- **Squeeze** some of the slime in one hand. Does it feel **firm**? What happens if you open your hand?
- **Roll** some of the slime between your hands into a ball. Drop it back into the bowl. How does it **land**?

When you squeeze, hit or roll the mixture, the cornflour particles clump together. That's why it seems SOLID.

But if you move the mixture gently or leave it to rest, the particles slide over each other. This makes it look and feel like a LIQUID.

And there you have it! Slime isn't just silly – it's scientific too!

ACKNOWLEDGEMENTS

I feel so grateful and a little overwhelmed to be writing acknowledgments for the sixth book in the series. There is an amazing team who support and guide me on this journey and I don't think I can ever really express how much I appreciate them. Kate Shaw, my wonderful agent, who keeps me moving forward, always. Special thanks also to the team at ILA who do work in the background that I don't see but I know it's happening and I'm so grateful for all your support.

I knew when I signed with the team at Usborne that I had found a very special home for Anisha and that is as true now as it was six books ago. My love and thanks to my editors, Stephanie and Alice and to all the team there who pour their passion and expertise into every book.

What can I say about working with Emma McCann except that it has been a joy and so inspiring which only grows greater with time.

I must also say thank you to author friends I've made along the way, as well as teachers, librarians, festival organisers, booksellers and bloggers. Your support has made all of this feel like a dream.

And finally, all my love to my family and friends. You keep me grounded, you give me lots of material for stories and you fill my heart up with so much joy and laughter.

MEET THE AUTHOR

Name: Serena Kumari Patel

Lives with: My brilliant family, Deepak, Alyssa and Reiss

Favourite Subjects: Science and History

Ambitions: To learn to ride a bike (I never learned as a kid).

To keep trying things I'm scared of.

To write lots more books.

Most embarrassing moment:

Singing in Hindi at a talent show and getting most of the words wrong. I hid in the loo after!

MEET THE ILLUSTRATOR

Name: Emma Jane McCann

Lives with: A mysterious Tea Wizard called Granny Goddy, a family of bats in the attic, and far too many spiders. (I promise I'm not a witch.)

Favourite thing to draw: Spooky stuff like Dracula's Den in Anisha's first adventure. (Still not a witch, honest.)

Ambitions: To master a convincing slow foxtrot.

Most embarrassing moment:

I used to collect old teacups and china. One day, I was in a teashop with a friend and the cup she was using was really pretty. I picked it up to check the maker's mark on the base, forgot it already had tea in it, and spilled the lot all over the both of us. (Witches are too cool to ever do anything like that.)

Keep an eye out for news on
further adventures with
ANISHA, ACCIDENTAL DETECTIVE,
more from **SERENA PATEL,**
and fabulously funny stories at
www.usborne.com/fiction

@Usborne
@usborne_books
facebook.com/usbornepublishing